$_A$ Big Year
$_{for}$ Lily

THE ADVENTURES OF LILY LAPP

Book Three

A Big Year for Lily

Mary Ann Kinsinger and Suzanne Woods Fisher

Revell

a division of Baker Publishing Group
Grand Rapids, Michigan

© 2013 by Suzanne Woods Fisher and Mary Ann Kinsinger

Published by Revell
a division of Baker Publishing Group
P.O. Box 6287, Grand Rapids, MI 49516-6287
www.revellbooks.com

Printed in the United States of America

Library of Congress Cataloging-in-Publication Data
Kinsinger, Mary Ann.
    A big year for Lily / Mary Ann Kinsinger and Suzanne Woods Fisher.
       pages cm. — (The adventures of Lily Lapp ; book 3)
    Summary: "Continues the story of Amish Lily, her brothers, and her parents as she goes to school, makes new friends, and helps her mother and father as the family grows"—Provided by publisher.
    ISBN 978-0-8007-2134-3 (pbk.)
    1. Amish—Juvenile fiction. [1. Amish—Fiction. 2. Family life—Pennsylvania—Fiction. 3. Schools—Fiction. 4. Friendship—Fiction. 5. Pennsylvania—Fiction.] I. Fisher, Suzanne Woods. II. Title.
PZ7.K62933Bi 2013
[Fic]—dc23   2013005624

Scripture quotations, whether quoted or paraphrased, are from the King James Version of the Bible.

Published in association with Joyce Hart of The Hartline Literary Agency, LLC.

Illustrations by Tim Foley

13   14   15   16   17   18   19   7   6   5   4   3   2   1

From Mary Ann

I would like to dedicate this book
to my loving husband
who has given me unmeasured love and support.

From Suzanne

To my very special nephews—
Tim, Connor, Drew, and Scott.
I have a hunch you would each pick
Aaron Yoder as your favorite character!

Contents

Effie's Trick

*L*ily's toes felt tingly. She had been sitting on a backless church bench all morning long, and she wasn't sure how she could sit still one more moment. It was one hundred degrees in the shade, hotter inside the house. She wanted to swing her feet to wake them up, to jump up and down and stomp on them, but that wouldn't do at all. Mama would frown. There was a time and a place for all things, Mama often said. And church was a time to be still and silent. For three long hours. Even on a steamy July morning.

Lily glanced at baby Paul, snuggled in Mama's lap, looking at a little picture book of bunnies. It must be fun to be a baby and be held in church instead of having to sit on a hard bench until her back ached and her toes went dead. It was too bad she couldn't remember being a baby.

David Yoder, the minister, stood before the congregation, reciting some Bible verses in German that she couldn't understand. She stifled a yawn as her gaze shifted to an open window. A gentle breeze blew the white curtain. It reminded Lily of Mama's sheets on the clothesline, luffing in the wind. A lazy bumblebee flew inside and buzzed around David Yoder's long crinkly beard. He kept on solemnly preaching while the bee buzzed around him. Even the bee grew bored and flew back out the window. For a moment, Lily imagined what might have happened if the bee had stung David Yoder. Now *that* would have caused a little excitement!

At long last, David Yoder's voice flattened to a deep hum—a sign that the long sermon was coming to an end. Around her, Lily noticed others shift their bottoms on the hard bench in anticipation of the end. The final hymn was sung and church was over! As soon as the fellowship meal was over, Lily could have the rest of the afternoon to play with her friends.

Mama asked Lily to take care of baby Paul while she went to help the other women set stacks of homemade bread on the tables and pour fresh peppermint tea into cups. Lily didn't mind taking care of baby Paul. All her friends eagerly took turns holding him, and it made her feel special to know that she had something other girls wanted.

When lunch was ready, everyone sat at long tables to eat the bread and sip their tea. The bread was spread with a special sweetened creamy peanut butter—church peanut butter. The cookie tray was piled high with Ida Kauffman's sugar cookies and Mama's raisin-filled cookies. Lily watched the raisin-filled cookies disappear as the tray made its way down toward the end, where she and Mama sat. She had worried there wouldn't be enough and even gave Mama a tiny suggestion to bring more cookies along this morning. Mama said there would be plenty, but Lily knew that everybody loved Mama's raisin-filled cookies. Only two cookies were left on the tray as it passed by Ida and Effie Kauffman. Ida didn't take a raisin-filled cookie and shook her head when Effie tried to grab one. Instead, they took a bland sugar cookie. There were plenty of those on the tray.

That left two raisin-filled cookies for Lily and Cousin Hannah. As Lily nibbled on her cookie, she tried to pay attention to Mama and Aunt Mary's conversation, but she thought it was uninteresting. All mothers ever seemed to talk about was the work they had done that week and what silly new thing their babies had learned to do. She was glad when the bishop announced it was time to have a prayer of thanks. Finally, Lily could go play.

Lily and Hannah hurried to join their friends. Beth suggested they could play church with their dolls but Effie Kauffman said no. "Church is at my house today so I get to pick what we play," Effie said, sounding very much like Ida, her bossy mother. "Besides, we're in fourth grade now. Much too old to play with dolls."

Lily and the other girls looked at each other, eyes wide. None of them thought that they were too old, at the age of nine, to play with dolls. They loved to play with their dolls! No one dared to speak up, though. As Papa had once pointed out, Effie ruled the henhouse.

"Then what do you want to do?" Beth asked Effie.

"I think we'll go on a walk like the big girls often do on Sunday afternoons," Effie said. "It's a very grown-up thing to do." She started out the door and up a hill behind the house to a little orchard. Four little girls, including Lily, trotted behind her.

The orchard did look pretty, the trees full with soft green leaves. Lily spotted a few apple trees that were loaded with ripening apples.

"Perhaps," Effie said, tapping a finger on her chin, "perhaps we could each pick an apple."

Lily grew suspicious. It was not like Effie to be generous, even with an apple on a tree. Beth and Malinda walked around the tree to decide which apple they wanted to eat. Lily had already found the one she wanted. Near the top was one of the most beautiful apples she had ever seen. It was enormous, bright yellow, and Lily could practically taste the crisp juicy crunch as she bit into it.

She pointed it out to Hannah. There must be some way to get to it. "I have an idea," Lily said. "I'll go ask Joseph to climb the tree and get that apple for us." Joseph was always climbing trees.

"No boys," Effie said, which made Lily annoyed. Effie was always adding new rules onto her games.

"I could climb the tree," Hannah said.

"Girls don't climb trees," Effie said. "That's sinful. Everybody knows that."

Hannah looked bewildered. "It is not sinful to climb a tree," Lily blurted out.

Beth, Malinda, and Hannah's mouths opened to a surprised O. They seemed astonished to hear Lily stand up to Effie. It just wasn't done.

It sure did feel good, though. It sure did. Lily ignored her friends' warning looks and kept going. "It might not be ladylike but it is *not* sinful. I'm going to climb up and get that apple myself." She grasped the lowest branch and pulled herself up. She looked down at the girls and took in the varied expressions on their faces: Effie looked angry, Malinda seemed worried, and Beth was amused. Best of all, Hannah looked pleased. That was all the encouragement Lily needed. She scrambled to the next branch, then the next, until she reached the branch that held the big shiny apple. She gathered the corners of her apron together to make a basket and dropped her apple into it. She picked a few more apples for the girls. The biggest sweetest apples always grew near the top of the tree. Everybody knew *that*.

With five apples in her apron, Lily clutched it with her left hand and made her way back down the tree. When she had reached the last branch, she carefully tossed the apples, one by one, to the girls. Lily took a big bite of the apple she'd been after. Delicious! Crisp and juicy, just like she imagined.

As Lily hopped down, her dress caught on a branch and held. For a split second, she dangled in the air. Then a ripping sound filled the air and she dropped the rest of the way to the ground. Effie laughed hysterically as the girls helped Lily to her feet. "Oh Lily, your dress!" Hannah said.

Lily's heart sank. Her dress had ripped in a huge three-cornered tear. Her beautiful purple dress was ruined.

The nice big apple no longer seemed quite so delicious. There was nothing to do but try to hold the tear shut and go find Mama. She wished she had never climbed that tree. Mama would be disappointed that she had torn her best Sunday dress.

As Lily entered the house, clutching the backside of her torn dress, the women stopped talking. Everyone stared at Lily. She wished she could disappear. Mama quickly came to her side and guided her into a bedroom. "What happened?" she asked.

"I climbed a tree to get some apples," Lily said. "My dress caught on a little branch when I jumped down."

Ida Kauffman had followed them into the bedroom and listened to Lily's confession. She handed Mama some safety pins to try to hold Lily's skirt together. "That's what happens when you try to draw attention to yourself," she said to Lily. "God has to teach you a lesson." Before she left the room, she turned back for a moment, one eyebrow arched. "Wi der Baum, so die Frucht. Recht, Rachel?" *Such as the tree is, such is the fruit. Isn't that true, Rachel?*

Mama kept her eyes down. After Ida left, Mama asked Lily, "Why on earth would you climb a tree in your Sunday clothes?"

"I wasn't planning to," Lily said. "But Effie said that it's sinful for girls to climb trees. Next thing I knew I was halfway up the tree."

Mama finished pinning Lily's skirt. Then she put her hands on Lily's shoulders. "I know how it can feel to want to prove someone wrong. But when you act on that prideful impulse, it usually hurts you in the end. Next time, think twice, Lily." She tapped her gently on the nose and rose to leave.

Lily was surprised that Mama understood how it felt to want to prove someone wrong. She wondered if that someone for Mama might be Ida Kauffman. Maybe there was hope for Lily after all. If Mama had grown up to be good and sweet and kind even when people annoyed her, maybe someday Lily would, too.

In the meantime, Effie Kauffman made life a misery.

Bats in the Bedroom

$\mathcal{L}$ily loved her new bedroom. When the family first moved into the ugly olive-green house, over a year ago, the upstairs hallway had doubled as her bedroom. Joseph and Dannie galloped past her bed every time they ran to their room. Every sound in the kitchen floated up the stairs and to her room. The hallway bedroom had been a sore trial for Lily.

But just after school had let out for the summer, Papa had finished off a special room for Lily up in the attic. And now she had the best room in the house.

The window was Lily's favorite part of her bedroom. She pretended it was a picture frame, changing throughout the day and night. Mama had made a fluffy white curtain for it but Lily liked to keep the curtain drawn back so she could look out at the tall pine trees. The breeze that swept through the pine branches sounded like whispers to Lily. Sometimes, when she lay in bed, she wondered what they might be saying to each other, if trees could talk.

She could see the rolling mountains far off in the distance from her window. The mountains changed color throughout the day and night. They went from pinks and lavenders at dawn to blues and greens at dusk. In the night, she could see the moon travel across the sky.

The walls were a soft honey color made from smoothly varnished maple boards. In one corner, Papa had built a closet. It was nice to have her dresses hanging neatly inside of it instead of on a hook on the wall. Mama had painted the plywood floor lavender and made a bright purple rag rug to use beside her bed.

The rug matched the pretty purple cushion Mama had made for the chair beside the bed. A long, low chest of drawers stood along another wall. Grandma had crocheted a lavender doily for Lily's little oil lamp to stand on. And Grandpa had built a pretty bookshelf for her books and made a small nightstand for her bedside. Lily kept a flashlight on top in case she woke during the night.

Tonight, after she got ready for bed, Lily pulled her diary from its special hiding place—far from the eyes of curious little brothers. She wrote a few paragraphs about her day and tucked it away again. As she crossed the room to blow out her lamp, she paused by the window to gaze at the moon, a tiny sliver above the distant mountains. If she squinted her eyes, it almost looked like a cookie with a big bite out of it.

She climbed into bed, pulled the covers up under her chin, and closed her eyes. Everything about her room made her feel happy.

Lily's eyes flew open. Her heart pounded like a drum. There was a strange noise in her bedroom. She held her breath and tried to listen. There it was again! A rustling flapping bumping noise. Something was *in* her room! Her hands trembled as she reached over to get the flashlight. She flashed the light around her room and found the sound: a bat fluttered about her room, darting and diving, trying to find its way back out.

Lily quickly ducked and pulled her covers over her head. She heard the bat fly around and around her room. She couldn't stay in this room for one minute longer. She jumped out of bed, holding her pillow over her head, dashed out of her room, and flew down the stairs to knock on Papa and Mama's bedroom door.

"Who is it?" Papa sounded sleepy.

"It's me," Lily said. "There's a bat in my bedroom."

Papa opened the door. "There's a bat in your bedroom? What does it look like?"

"It looks like an ugly little mouse with wings. And it keeps flying into the walls."

"Wait here while I get something to catch it." Papa put his boots on by the kitchen door and went out into the dark night. A few minutes later, he came back inside with the buggy whip. He told her to stay put as he went upstairs. Lily wondered how Papa could catch the bat with a buggy whip. She had never even seen him use the whip. It had been carried in the little whip holder outside the buggy as long as she could remember. She thought he didn't know how to use it.

Lily's curiosity got the best of her. She tiptoed up the stairs and opened the door to her bedroom a tiny crack so she could watch. Papa stood in the middle of the room watching the bat. It flew back and forth across her room, bumping into the walls, trying to find a way to get out. Papa snapped the whip lightning fast and the bat fell to the floor. Lily clasped her hand over her mouth to keep from squealing out loud. Papa bent down and gingerly picked the bat up by the tip of one of its wings. Lily hurried down the stairs and waited for him.

"Did you kill it?" she asked when he came downstairs.

"No. I didn't intend to. The whip knocked it out for a little bit, but it will wake up soon. Bats are helpful little creatures as long as they don't get inside the house. They eat mosquitoes."

Lily shuddered. The bat looked hideous to her. She would rather get a few mosquito bites than have a bat in her bedroom again.

Lily waited to go back to bed until Papa double-checked her bedroom to make sure that there were no more bats. Then she climbed into bed and fell sound asleep.

For an entire week, no bats came to visit Lily's room. She'd settled into a peaceful sleep one night when she suddenly woke, startled to hear the same bat-like flutters and bumps. She flew downstairs to get Papa.

This time, she waited downstairs while Papa knocked the bat unconscious with the buggy whip. Again, Papa double-checked her room for bats before she would go back into it.

The next morning, Papa went to inspect her room. "I need to see if I can find how these bats are getting into your room. This has to stop."

Lily couldn't agree more. It was horrible to wake up in the middle of the night because a creepy bat flew around her bedroom. What if the bat flew right at her? What if it touched her? Or bit her? Just thinking of its mousy little face made her shudder.

Papa examined every inch of the walls and ceiling, but he couldn't find any cracks big enough for a bat to squeeze through. "I can't figure it out," he said, shaking his head. "I don't know how they're getting into your room. Hopefully, that's the end of it."

And it was. Until the next week, when another bat found its way into Lily's bedroom. Two days after that, another one.

Papa had had enough. If he couldn't find a way to stop the bats from getting into Lily's bedroom, he decided she would have to move out of her pretty little attic bedroom. At first, Lily thought that meant she would have to go back to having a bedroom in the hallway. How sad!

But Papa had built a nice big addition to the house, and he and Mama already had planned to move their bedroom into what used to be the old kitchen. They would give Lily their old bedroom. "The bats only moved up the timetable," he said. Papa spent that Saturday moving all the furniture from one room to another.

Lily was sad to leave her pretty attic bedroom. It was private and away from little brothers, and it had a purple floor. Her new bedroom was on the second floor, near the stairs, and she would hear the boys clomping up and down. On the other hand, there were no bats in this new bedroom and that was a definite plus. She still had her pretty purple rug and cushion. Another plus.

That night, as Lily got ready for bed, she looked around her bedroom. It wasn't nearly as pretty. There was ugly green-and-brown striped wallpaper on the walls. The floor was dark blue linoleum with big red swirls all over it. It almost made Lily feel dizzy to look at it. Looking out the window wasn't much fun. The pine trees that had seemed so tall and majestic in her attic bedroom only blocked her view of the distant mountains. But she could still hear their whispers. That was a good thing.

As she lay in bed, she thought about her pretty attic room. She wondered if it felt sad and empty without her. Did things have feelings? She would have to ask Papa, she thought, yawning.

Since bats slept throughout the day, maybe she could play in the room during the day! It would be a fine place to play with her dolls or read a book. Whenever Cousin Hannah or Beth came to play, they would have a perfect place to play and not worry about being bothered by little brothers. She yawned again.

With plans on her mind to turn her attic room into a play-room, during the daytime only, Lily drifted off to sleep.

CHAPTER

3

A Walk in the Woods

On a warm July afternoon, when the air felt still, Papa came into the kitchen to talk to Mama. "Jim needs new horseshoes. I'm going to take him over to the black-smith." He glanced at Lily and smiled. "I thought Lily might like to go along and play with Beth while her father works on Jim's shoes."

Mama smiled. "I think Lily might be persuaded to go with you."

"Oh yes!" Lily was excited to hear that she could play with Beth. She didn't get to see Beth often during the summer. She wouldn't even mind helping Beth with her chores.

Lily yanked her bonnet off its hook and ran to sit on the buggy seat while Papa hitched Jim to the buggy. Soon, they were off.

As soon as Jim pulled into the Rabers' driveway, Beth flew out of the house, surprised to see Lily seated next to Papa.

The two girls followed Papa as he unhitched Jim from the buggy and led him to a shady tree next to the barn. Jonas, Beth's father, plucked a big, heavy, black leather apron from a peg inside the barn door and tied it around his waist. He carried a wooden toolbox filled with nails, files, clippers, hammers, and horseshoes of different sizes.

Before Jonas got to work on Jim's feet, he made friends with the horse, which Lily thought was very smart. Jonas walked up to Jim and talked to him a little and stroked his neck. Then he picked up his front hoof. He held it firmly between his legs as he reached into the toolbox for a hammer and pulled Jim's old metal horseshoe off. Next, he took a big pair of clippers and clipped some of the hoof off.

"Does that hurt Jim?" Lily asked.

"No, it feels the same as clipping your toenails," Papa said. "Jim's hooves need to be trimmed regularly so he doesn't stumble when he walks."

Jonas picked up a file and started to file Jim's big hoof. Jonas's big German Shepherd dog, Bumper, came over to see what was happening. He sniffed at the bits of hoof clippings and started to chew on one. *Disgusting*, Lily thought.

Beth leaned over to whisper in Lily's ear. "Let's go play."

The girls ran to a swing under a big maple tree in front of the house. They took turns pushing each other, stopping between turns to tell each other important news.

"Baby Paul is starting to crawl," Lily said. "He tries to put everything into his mouth." Just like that dog, Bumper. *Disgusting*, Lily thought.

It was Beth's turn. "I think my brother has a crush on Katie Miller. His ears turn red whenever he sees her at church."

My, that was interesting. Much more interesting than Paul's

crawling. Lily was going to have to keep her ears open for better news.

Much too soon, Papa came looking for Lily. "Time to go home," he said. "Jim has four new shoes and is ready to try them out."

Lily hopped off the swing. "We just got started playing. Could I stay a little longer? I could walk home over the fields by myself. It isn't far."

Papa lifted his hat and ran his fingers through his hair. "Beth might have something she needs to do."

"I'd like Lily to stay," Beth said. The girls held their breath, waiting to hear Papa's answer.

"Go ask your father, Beth, and see if it would be okay with him," Papa said.

Lily and Beth ran to find Jonas Raber in the barn, putting away his leather apron and toolbox. Lily explained that she wanted to stay a little longer and then walk home by herself. "Do you mind?"

"I don't mind," Jonas said, smiling. A person couldn't help but smile back when Jonas Raber smiled. His teeth stuck out in all different directions, a real assortment, and his eyes were warm and kind.

Lily ran to find Papa; Beth skipped along behind her. "I can stay!"

"Be a good girl," Papa said. "And remember to come home before too late." He climbed up on the buggy and gave Jim a *tch-tch* sound. Jim trotted down the drive with an extra spring in his step, proud of his new shoes.

Lily turned to Beth. "Now we can swing all day." But after a few more turns on the swing, the girls grew bored and tried to think of something else to do.

"Have you seen my little playhouse?" Beth asked. "Dad made it for my birthday."

The girls ran to the edge of the garden. Beside the garden gate was the cutest little playhouse Lily had ever seen. Beth held the door open and Lily ducked her head to step inside.

In the middle of the tiny room sat a small table and two little chairs. On one wall were several shelves filled with old pots and pans and chipped dishes that Beth's mother no longer used.

"Let's get some carrots and cucumbers from the garden," Beth said. In the garden, they picked several small cucumbers.

They rubbed their aprons over the cucumbers to remove the prickles, just like their mothers did. Next came the carrots. This took a little more work: they held the carrot tops in their fists to get a better look at the small top of orange carrot that peeped above the ground. They didn't want a carrot that was too big or too little. The big ones tasted bitter and the tiny ones tasted watery. It was important to find the right-sized carrot—those were the ones that tasted the best: nice and sweet, crunchy and carroty. After they pulled all the carrots they wanted, Beth filled a pail with water from the springhouse by the barn. They took turns carrying it back to the playhouse. Water sloshed out of the pail and splashed against their skirts and over their bare feet. They didn't mind. It felt good on such a hot day.

In the playhouse, Beth filled one of the pots on the shelf with water. They swished their carrots in the water until the dirt had been rinsed off.

Beth set the table while Lily divided the carrots and cucumbers on the plates. Then they sat down to eat and tried to have an important, grown-up conversation. With a terribly stern and serious face, Beth brought up the worry of raising youth in this day and age, which made Lily giggle. Then Lily would try: she would make her face stop smiling, then purse her lips and discuss the behavior of the youth in church lately and had Beth noticed a lot of winking going on between the boys and the girls? With that, the girls were overcome by a giggling fit. They didn't even have to say it out loud: they were both imitating Ida Kauffman as she paid visits to their mothers! Lily was laughing so hard that her tummy hurt.

"Let's pretend to bake cakes," Beth said. "We can fill some pans with wet sand and then decorate them with flowers and leaves to make them pretty."

They rinsed the dishes they had used and set them back up on the shelf. Then they went to get sand from the sandbox, added water until it felt just right and ran to find flowers. They filled their aprons with bright yellow buttercups and sweet purple clover blossoms. They were so busy decorating their little sand cakes that both of them were startled when Beth's mother stepped out on the porch and called, "Beth! Suppertime."

Lily was shocked! She had been having so much fun that she had forgotten all about watching the time. She had told Papa she wouldn't stay too late and the sun was already low in the sky. "I have to go home right now!"

Lily hurried down the driveway, too worried to even wave goodbye to Beth. She walked down the road until she came to a little shortcut that led through the woods. She thought it was the shortcut Joseph liked to use, but it looked different in the late afternoon light.

She gave a start, her heart leaping in fright. A sudden noise, a small crashing sound—something in the bushes. It sounded big. It sounded huge.

Lily didn't dare look around. What if it were a black bear? She had just heard a story about a farmer meeting up with a bear in his cornfield. She heard another sound. It was coming closer. Instinct took over and she started to run. Faster and faster! She had never run so fast in her life. Her lungs hurt from running so hard. Her side ached and her legs felt as if they could buckle beneath her. She simply couldn't run one more step. She stopped to catch her breath.

Crunch, pop, snap. Something was following her. What if it were a mountain lion? Joseph was always talking about mountain lions in the woods. The noise got closer and closer. She started to shake, so frightened that she couldn't budge.

Right behind her, a bush crackled. She squawked and flung her arms over her head. She was going to be eaten alive!

A little cottontail darted in the underbrush beside the path. Every hop it made caused twigs and dry leaves to crunch and snap. Lily was relieved! And then, embarrassed. She had been running from a cute little bunny.

Lily walked a little farther and came to the edge of the woods. There, across the field, was her house. A buttery light glowed from the kitchen. Lily had never been so glad to see that little ugly olive-green house. She ran up to the porch and into the kitchen. Stirring a pot on the stove top, Mama spun around. A look of relief swept over her face when she saw Lily.

Papa was washing up at the sink. He didn't look very happy with Lily. "We were getting worried about you. I was almost ready to go looking for you."

"I'm sorry, Papa," Lily said and slid into her chair at the table. "I forgot to pay attention to the time. As soon as I realized how late it was, I ran all the way home. I thought a bear or a mountain lion was chasing me, but it was only a little bunny." As soon as the words left her mouth, she wished them back.

Joseph and Dannie looked at each other, jaws opened wide, then they doubled up with laughter. "Only a girl would think a bunny is a bear!" Joseph said, between fits of laughter.

"Only a girl!" Dannie echoed, like he always did.

Even baby Paul started to giggle, which got Papa and Mama grinning.

Lily's face grew hot, as if she were standing too close to Mama's stove. She was humiliated. She didn't think any of them understood how frightening a bunny could sound in the dark woods.

Lily's Perfect Day Unravels

There was a little less evening now in late August, a warning of summer's end. Joseph took that warning to heart and was determined to live every day twice over before he lost his freedom to the schoolhouse. Lily thought he was being dramatic. She couldn't understand how anyone couldn't like school. Joseph kept himself scarce from the house, where Mama was sewing up a storm of new school clothes.

The first day of school came on a beautiful sunny morning. Lily could hardly wait. She held the silky white curtain back with one hand as she stood by the living room window, waiting for her cousins, Levi and Hannah, to walk down the road. All summer long, Lily had looked forward to having Levi and Hannah join school.

Bong, bong, bong . . . She turned and glanced at the clock. Eight bongs. What if Hannah and Levi were late? It would be terrible to be late on the very first day of school. Lily peered out the window and breathed a sigh of relief as she saw Levi and Hannah round the bend. Lily grabbed her bonnet and lunch pail and darted out the door. She tossed a goodbye over her shoulder to Mama.

Joseph was outside, swinging on the porch swing. He was trying to squeeze every last drop out of summer, not at all excited about school starting. Lily did not understand that brother of hers. Slowly, he picked up his lunch box and trailed behind Lily to the end of the driveway. They waited for Levi and Hannah to catch up to them.

The first thing that went through Lily's mind was that Hannah's new purple dress was much prettier than her own brown one. But she knew what Mama would have to say about that:

Lily, can't you think about how wonderful it is to have your cousin here instead of what you are wearing?

Yes, Mama.

But she couldn't. She wanted Hannah's purple dress. "Hannah, are you excited for school?" Lily asked.

"Not really," Hannah said. "I want to help my mother bake pies and cookies today. And I'd rather play outside than have to sit at a desk all day."

That was shocking news to Lily. Baking cookies and pies was fine but then came washing dishes. Lots and lots of dishes. Besides, how could anyone not love school? She reminded herself that Hannah hadn't attended school in two years, and the last teacher she'd had was Teacher Katie . . . who was horrible. "School is lots and lots of fun. We get to learn new things. Teacher Rhoda is a very nice teacher. We play with our friends at recess. We can read library books when we get done with all our lessons. And we get to eat special lunches that Mama packs every day. Best of all, we don't have to wash dishes."

Lily skipped a few steps. "I like helping Mama work, but school is so much more fun." She didn't think that now was the time to mention two individuals who made school very stressful: Effie Kauffman and Aaron Yoder. At any given moment, Lily could be minding her own business and one or the other would create some horrible mischief that was often targeted at her. "This year will be even better. You're here! We're both in fourth grade so we'll get to sit together, eat together, have recess together." In other words, Effie and Aaron wouldn't bother Lily as much. Naturally, she didn't say that to Hannah. There would be plenty of time for the terrible truth.

"What are you having for lunch today?" Hannah asked.

Lily opened her lunch box and peered inside. "I'm having a sandwich, a banana, and two oatmeal raisin cookies. What's in your lunch?"

Hannah opened her lunch pail, frowning. "Carrot sticks and an egg sandwich." She snapped the lid to her lunch box shut again.

Uh-oh. Carrot sticks were a problem. Too crunchy. Aaron Yoder often teased Lily when she had carrot sticks in her lunch. "Egg sandwiches are my favorite." She tried to encourage Hannah, but that lunch of hers was a worry. Levi's bragging was another worry. He never missed a chance to puff himself up.

By the time the two girls arrived at school, almost all the other children were already there. The first thing Lily wanted to do was to find her desk. She hoped, hoped, hoped that, this year, Aaron Yoder would not be sitting right across the aisle from her.

Lily found her desk and then looked at the desk across the aisle. "Hannah, come look!"

Hannah hurried over to see her name on a small tag. Lily

was so happy. The school year was starting out well. Hannah would sit right next to her. No Aaron Yoder!

The girls set to work arranging their new pencils and school supplies in their desks. Then they checked name tags on the other desks. Lily read the one behind hers and groaned. "Noooooooo!"

Hannah looked up. "What's wrong?"

"Aaron Yoder is sitting right behind me." How awful. She didn't want to sit right in front of that terrible boy all year long.

But then she brightened. She wouldn't have to actually look at Aaron, unless she turned around, and she decided she would never, ever do that. Aaron was invisible to her.

"Children, time to come in!" Teacher Rhoda rang the bell on the school steps and the students scrambled to find their seats. As soon as the class settled down, Teacher Rhoda read a Bible story. And then the new school term began.

Lily opened one of her brand-new books and admired how crisp and clean the pages were. She hoped she could keep it looking nice all year long.

"Fourth grade," Teacher Rhoda said, "work on assignment one in your math workbook."

The first assignment of the year! Lily got right to work. It was so good to be back in school and even better to be a fourth grader. She wiggled happily in her seat and picked up her pencil, but it slipped through her fingers and dropped on the floor. She bent down to retrieve it. As she pulled herself up, her head bumped against something. She couldn't sit up—something was pressing down on the back of her head. She glanced behind her and saw Aaron Yoder with a big goofy grin on his face. He was holding his hand above her head. Lily ducked out of his reach and sat straight up, furious. She reached up to check her prayer covering and try to pouf it where Aaron had squashed it. How infuriating!

Lily glanced over at Hannah, embarrassed and mad. At least, this year, she had an ally against the monkeyshine of Aaron Yoder. But Hannah sat there with a big smile on her face, as if it was funny!

Anger flooded through Lily. "It's not funny!" she snapped at Hannah, and her cousin's smile faded.

This was only the first day of school and already Aaron was being difficult. And Hannah was not being an ally at all. Despite Lily's rule to never turn around in her desk, she turned around. She meant to stick her tongue out at Aaron, but as she turned, her elbow hit her brand-new book on top of her desk and knocked it to the floor. Before she could pick it up, Aaron put his dirty bare foot on it.

Teacher Rhoda noticed. She came back to their seats to see what the commotion was all about. "Aaron, get your foot off of Lily's book," she said sternly. Aaron slowly lifted his foot and tucked it back under his desk while Lily picked her book up. She looked at it sadly. It had Aaron's big, dirty bare footprint on it. He was an awful boy.

The morning melted away. By midafternoon, an autumn haze drifted across the stifling schoolroom. Lily was relieved when school was dismissed. What a disappointing day. She plucked her bonnet from the hook at the back of the schoolhouse, pulled her lunch pail off the shelf, and headed out the door with Hannah.

Levi and Joseph started to run, but Lily didn't feel like running home from school. She trudged alongside of Hannah.

"I take back every bad thing I ever thought about school," Hannah said in a far-off voice. She had a strange dreamy look on her face and Lily worried if she might be getting sick. "Isn't Aaron Yoder the most wonderful boy in school?"

Wonderful? *Wonderful?* Why, Lily was just this moment thinking he was the worst boy in the state. The world. The universe.

Hannah swung her lunch pail at her side. "He can run faster than any of the other boys at school. And his eyes are such a pretty blue and his hair so nice and curly." She sighed a little. "Lily, do you think he likes me?"

Lily stopped in her tracks. "Why would you want him to like you? He isn't nice to any girls. Didn't you see what he did to my covering?" Her black covering was still squashed. "And don't forget my book." How terrible! To have to live with Aaron Yoder's dirty footprint on her beautiful new book, all year long. "And his hair looks like a wren has moved in and is building a nest."

Hannah giggled. "You should have seen how surprised you looked when you couldn't sit up because he was holding his hand above your head." She giggled harder. "It was so funny!"

Why was Hannah sticking up for Aaron? Lily shot her a look of irritation.

"You were right, Lily. School is exciting," Hannah said. "And the best part is that Aaron Yoder sits across the aisle from me, and I can look at him whenever I want to."

Lily shook her head in despair. How sad. Poor Cousin Hannah. She had been without school for so long that she had lost all logic.

All of Lily's wonderful plans for this school year were evaporating, like a wisp of steam over a teacup. She was so sure that everything would be better this year with Cousin Hannah by her side. Instead, everything was worse.

A Trip to Town

*L*ily was feeding baby Paul cereal in his high chair and getting very frustrated. He waved his arms and kicked his feet, demanding, "More, more!" He never stopped eating, that baby. She couldn't feed him fast enough. She glanced out the window to see if Papa had already put the harness on Jim and hitched him to the buggy. Papa was going to town today and had asked Lily if she wanted to go along. Of course! Of course she did.

"More, more!"

Lily turned her attention back to feeding the baby. She filled the spoon halfway and dodged Paul's waving hands to feed him another bite. Lily could hardly hold still, she was that excited. She had gone to town only once since they had moved to Pennsylvania. She knew Papa would wait patiently for her, but she still wished that Paul could be done with his breakfast. She tried giving him bigger and bigger bites, hoping his tummy would finally be full.

When the last spoonful was scraped from the bowl, Lily decided Paul had eaten enough for two babies. She lifted him out of the high chair and set him on the floor. He went toddling off to find his toys and Lily hurried to find her shoes and stockings. She wriggled her feet into them and stood up, feeling odd. She had been barefoot for months now, ever since late spring. Shoes felt heavy and clumsy. But it would never do to go barefoot to town.

Lily said goodbye to Mama and the boys and darted out the door. This was going to be a perfect day. Joseph and Dannie could help Mama with all the Saturday housecleaning. They could watch baby Paul while Lily enjoyed a long ride to town and back with Papa.

Papa was just tucking the tie rope under the seat as Lily hopped on the buggy. He gathered the reins in his hands, clucking "giddyup!" to Jim as he guided the horse out of the driveway and down the road.

It was a beautiful morning. Lily watched birds flit from branch to branch in the trees along the road. Leaves were starting to turn from green to orange, a hint that summer was ending and autumn was coming. The trees were so filled with heavy leaves that branches seemed to touch overhead. It seemed as if Lily and Papa were driving through a long tunnel. Sunlight peeked through the branches to light their way. A few squirrels darted around with nuts in their mouths. They were trying to find the perfect spot to bury them. Once winter came, if they could remember where they buried their nuts, they would dig them up. If they couldn't remember, a new tree would grow. Lily grinned.

She wondered how many trees along the road were once forgotten nuts.

As Jim trotted down the road, Papa started to whistle. The buggy went past neighbors' farms. Lily looked at the lazy cows, grazing or laying under trees, chewing their cuds. One or two would look over to watch them pass by, then go back to chewing. Horses were more interested in who passed by their fence. They would neigh to Jim, then canter alongside the fence, as if they had challenged him to a race. Lily knew that Jim would ignore them. He wouldn't even neigh back. *I have more important things to do today and don't have time to play your games,* Jim must have been thinking.

Lily sighed happily. She was sure there was no better place in the world to be than right there on the front seat of the buggy beside Papa. He asked about her first week of school. She told him everything: all she had learned, and even the part about Cousin Hannah thinking Aaron Yoder was so wonderful. "She doesn't know yet that he's the worst boy in school."

An amused look danced in Papa's eyes as she described her dilemma with Hannah and Aaron. But he didn't scold her for complaining about Aaron, or take Hannah's side. He just listened carefully. He was a fine listener, Papa was.

Too soon, they reached town. Papa guided Jim to the hitching post. They would walk to the stores and carry their things back to the buggy. Papa's first stop was the feed store to buy feed for Pansy the cow. For Jim, too. The clerk behind the counter added up the bill. As Papa counted out his money, the clerk told Lily she could pick out a lollipop.

Lily looked at all the lollipops and chose a purple one. She slipped it into her dress pocket hidden under her apron.

She hoped it would taste as good as it looked. Purple things usually did not disappoint.

Papa hoisted the bags of feed onto his shoulders, as if they were light as feather pillows, and walked back to the buggy. He set them in the back of the buggy and drew a shopping list out of his pocket.

"Next is a trip to the fabric store," he read. "Mama needs half a yard of denim to patch the boys' pants."

"I think boys have knees as hungry as their tummies," Lily said. "They always seem to have holes in their pants' knees. Mama says they have hollow tummies."

Papa laughed out loud. "Here I thought it was the grass they crawled on to play with their toys. All this time they had hungry knees. We'll have to tell Mama when we get home."

Lily was so pleased that Papa had laughed. She hadn't even known she was making a joke, and Papa had laughed! She couldn't stop grinning as she followed him inside the store. She stopped abruptly as her eyes took in the rows and rows of fabrics. All sorts of beautiful fabrics with flowers and other designs. She had never known there were such beautiful patterns. She spotted a pretty cream fabric sprinkled with tiny purple roses. Oh, wouldn't it be wonderful to have a dress in that fabric? She reached out to touch it. It felt nice and soft. Papa noticed. "Don't touch anything, Lily," he said.

Lily drew her hands away and held the sides of her apron so she wouldn't be tempted to touch more fabrics. But they were all so beautiful! Papa told the girl behind the counter what he wanted. Lily thought it was sad to buy only a piece of ugly denim when there were so many other pretty fabrics to choose from.

Papa paid for the denim and handed the bag to Lily. "Here, I'll let you carry this back to the buggy."

Lily tried to match her steps to Papa's long strides. He slowed down so she could keep up with him more easily. She chattered happily as they walked. She had so much to tell him! About how she was looking forward to seeing her friends in church tomorrow. About all the ideas she had for her friends to play after church was over. Lily hardly gave Papa a chance to answer anything before she launched into talking about something else. It was a wonder to her—to be able to talk to Papa without interruptions from any little brothers.

The next stop was the grocery store. Mama needed sugar and flour and a few other items. Lily pushed the cart for Papa up and down the aisles as he selected everything that Mama had written on the shopping list. Lily hoped Papa might buy some of the interesting things in the store instead of only the same old regular food that they always had. Store-bought cookies, for one. Puffy white marshmallows, for another. Sadly, Papa kept to Mama's list.

After Papa paid for the groceries, he handed Lily a light bag to hold while he carried everything else in his strong arms. Back at the hitching post, Jim waited patiently. Papa set the bags on the ground while he carefully stacked everything inside the buggy.

He took a big five gallon bucket out of the back of the buggy and popped the lid off. It was full of water. Lily watched as Papa lifted the pail up for Jim. Jim drank half of it and then gently blew the water droplets off his velvety nose to let Papa know that he had had enough. Papa dumped the rest of the water out on the street and put the pail back inside the buggy. He untied Jim, then paused and looked at Lily. "It's awfully warm today. How would you like to have an ice-cream cone?"

Of course she would! Of course. "Ice cream is one of my favorite things!"

Papa grinned and tied Jim back up. "Then let's go get you one."

Could this day get any better? Lily skipped happily beside Papa as they walked to a nearby ice cream shop. Papa ordered a big vanilla ice-cream cone and handed it to Lily. She admired the pile of swirled ice cream and then waited for Papa to give her a spoon to eat it. He turned to leave the store and she hurried to keep up with him. He must have forgotten that she would need a spoon.

"You'd better start eating it before it melts," Papa said as they walked back to the buggy.

"But how? I don't have a spoon."

"You don't need a spoon when you have a cone to hold the ice cream. You can lick it."

"Like a cat?"

Papa laughed. "Just like a cat."

Twice now, Papa had laughed! But Lily wasn't trying to be funny. She thought it seemed odd to lick ice cream. Tentatively, she tried it. *Oh my. Oh my goodness.* This was better than a spoon! She would never want a spoon for ice cream again. Licking was too much fun.

Papa held her cone as she climbed onto the buggy. Then he handed it back to her as he untied Jim. It was finally time to go home. The trip to town had gone much too fast.

Jim trotted up the road, Papa whistled merrily, and Lily quietly licked her ice cream. It was almost all gone except

for a few bites inside the cone. Her tongue couldn't reach the bottom. What a shame to let that ice cream melt. Here's where a spoon would have come in handy.

She tossed the cone out of the buggy. Maybe a squirrel or a bunny would come along and finish the last few bites of the ice cream.

Papa stopped whistling. "Why did you throw your cone away?"

"I couldn't lick the rest of the ice cream."

41

"The cone was something you could eat. And even if it wasn't, you shouldn't have thrown it out of the buggy."

Lily had thought the cone was made from cardboard. She was sorry she wasted it. She would always wonder what it would have tasted like. How sad.

But maybe Papa would take her to town again. And maybe he would buy her another ice-cream cone. Next time, she would eat the whole thing.

As Jim turned into Whispering Pines, with Papa whistling, Lily thought this was the most perfect day of her life. Thrown-out cone and all.

The Lesson of the Bumblebee

*C*loverdale was having an Indian summer—unusually warm days. Today was Aaron Yoder's birthday and he had brought in homemade soft pretzels as a treat. Salty pretzels. Under normal conditions, Lily would not accept anything from Aaron Yoder, but she had seen his mother deliver those pretzels, still warm, to Teacher Rhoda during first recess. Soft pretzels topped Lily's list for favorite treats. She tried to save part of her pretzel for lunch but it was too delicious. It made her thirsty, too. In fact, all of the children were thirsty after the pretzels. They lined up for a turn at the water pump and drank and drank to their hearts' content.

During lunch recess, Lily discovered a problem. A very, very serious problem. The girls' bathroom was not working. A small sign taped up to the door read Out of Order. Lily and her friends discussed using the boys' bathroom, but unanimously voted against it. Too many germs.

By the start of afternoon classes, Lily was in trouble. Just the sound of someone at the water pump made her remember how badly she needed to go to the girls' room. It became a very stressful situation. She crossed her legs. She squeezed her hands. She couldn't think of anything but getting to the bathroom. Fast.

It wasn't until the second recess that Teacher Rhoda went out to use the bathroom and discovered the sign. She pulled it off the wall and went inside. Lily and her friends ran over to wait for her to come out. "We thought the bathroom was broken," Lily said.

"Girls," Teacher Rhoda said, "think about it. First, it was a note written in a boy's handwriting. Second, what could possibly be out of order in an outhouse?"

Oh. *Oh!*

Out on the front porch, Papa dipped the little paintbrush into the jar of white paint. Now that Mama had finally chosen a name for the farmette, Papa was working on a sign. With careful, elegant strokes, he painted letters on the big green sign that sat on top of two wooden sawhorses. The sign would be posted at the end of their driveway. As he finished the letter N, Lily started to giggle. If Papa stopped now, the sign would read Whispering Pin. A whispering pin would be funny. Imagine all the things a pin could tell a person: "Oh my . . . her underwear is a little threadbare!" or "Goodness gracious, she is getting rather plump!"

Papa whistled a happy tune as he painted E and S to make it Whispering Pines. Then he started on smaller letters underneath the farmette's name. Lily hummed along quietly as she watched him. Joseph and Dannie had wandered off to play in the sandbox. They had been watching Papa paint but quickly grew bored. Lily was glad. She liked spending time alone with Papa.

As Papa dipped his paintbrush into the jar, a fat bumblebee circled and buzzed around Lily's head. She jerked away, but then the bee landed on a freshly painted letter. Its fuzzy black feet were covered in white paint. It walked across the sign and made tiny bee footprints across the green sign.

Lily wanted to swat it away but was afraid that she would ruin Papa's beautiful sign even more than the bumblebee already had.

"Look, Papa," she said. "A bumblebee is ruining your sign. It's making little white tracks over the green background."

Papa tried to shoo the bumblebee away but its feet seemed to be too heavy with paint to be able to fly. He reached into his pocket and got his big red handkerchief and carefully lifted the bumblebee off the sign. "There. Now it can't make any more tracks."

"But it ruined your sign," Lily said.

Papa only smiled. "I don't think anyone will notice those tracks unless they look closely." He dipped his paintbrush back into the jar of paint and started to paint another letter. "You know, Lily, the sign is a lot like the people we meet. If we want to find fault with it, we can look much closer and see things like those little tracks. In fact, by looking too closely, you'll notice that some of the letters aren't exactly perfect. If we focus on those little faults, we'll forget that the sign is actually a pretty good sign."

Papa put the paintbrush down. "I could brush some more green paint over those little tracks, but I think I'll just leave them. That way whenever you and I see this sign, it can remind us to focus on the good things in the people we meet instead of any little faults they might have."

Aaron Yoder and Effie Kauffman, he meant. Each day, Lily had come home from school with new complaints about Aaron and Effie. Perfectly reasonable complaints.

Papa kept on painting and before long, he was satisfied the sign was done. Whispering Pines was on the top in nice big letters, curved like a rainbow. In smaller letters underneath were the words, Solid Oak, Cherry, and Walnut Furniture.

"I'll go get the posts ready for our sign," Papa said. "Want to come with me?"

Lily quickly put her chair back inside the house and followed Papa to the end of the driveway. Joseph and Dannie dropped their toys in the sandbox and hurried to join them. They watched with interest as Papa used his posthole digger and shovel to dig two deep holes. Digging, apparently, was more interesting to little boys than painting. Once the holes were deep enough, Papa put a long post into each hole. As he held the posts straight, he asked the children to drop stones into the holes around the posts.

Once the posts stood straight without help, Papa threw in big shovelfuls of dirt until the holes were filled all the way to the top. He packed the dirt firmly, then tried to wiggle the posts. They didn't budge. Not an inch. And Papa was satisfied.

The next day, Papa carried the sign to the end of the driveway and nailed it to the posts. Mama planted a nice circle of pretty pink impatiens flowers around the signposts. Lily thought the whole thing looked beautiful.

She couldn't see those little white tracks the bumblebee had made but she knew they were there. She knew the sign would remind her to focus on the good in others. She hoped such thinking might work with Aaron Yoder and Effie Kauffman, but she doubted it.

The Sandwich Switch

*L*ily's tummy rumbled. She glanced up at the clock. Almost lunchtime. Teacher Rhoda noticed, too. "Put your books away for noon recess."

The students closed their books, placed them inside their desks, and stood quietly next to their seats. Teacher Rhoda drew out the first note of a song and the children joined in, singing of God's blessings.

Row by row, the children filed to the back of the school-house to wash their hands. Lily splashed cold water over her hands, dried them on a towel, and hurried to get her lunch box. She was especially hungry today. At her desk, she opened her lunch box and was surprised to discover that Mama had made a sandwich with store-bought bread and deli meat. Mama enjoyed putting special treats in Joseph and Lily's lunches. This was the best surprise!

Lily savored every bite until second grader Lavina Schrock pointed to her and said, "Lily Lapp is eating my sandwich!"

47

Lily paused mid-chew. She looked at Lavina's desk. There was a familiar-looking homemade whole wheat bread and egg sandwich. Lily looked over at Joseph. He was eating one of Mama's egg sandwiches.

Lily offered the half-eaten deli-meat-on-store-bought-bread sandwich back to Lavina but she didn't want it, nor did she want Lily's egg sandwich either. Effie had turned around in her desk and pinched her face up into a knot of exaggerated disgust.

"How did you get my sandwich?" Lavina said.

Effie Kauffman turned around to face them. She had to get involved in everything. *Everything.* "Lily must have stolen it from your lunch box."

"Effie, turn around in your seat and finish your lunch," Teacher Rhoda said. She looked at Lily. "After everyone is done eating, I want Lily to stay in for a little while."

How humiliating! Lily's heart sank. It was terrible to have to stay inside. Only troublemakers, like Aaron and Sam, stayed in during recess. She was sure that all the children assumed she had stolen Lavina's sandwich. She hadn't! Lily wanted to slap that smug smile right off Effie's face, but then she really would be in trouble. She had to bite on her lip to keep her eyes from filling up with tears as the children ran outside to play.

The only two people left in the schoolhouse were Lily and Teacher Rhoda. It felt eerily quiet.

"Tell me about the sandwich," Teacher Rhoda said in a kind voice. Not accusing, like Effie.

"It was in my lunch box," Lily said. "I just started eating it. I had no idea that it belonged to Lavina."

"How did it get into your lunch box?"

"I don't know," Lily said, her voice quivering. She wished her voice sounded more convincing.

"Have you ever wished you had someone else's lunch?"

"Yes. All the time." Was that the right answer? Yes? No? It was true that Lily had often wished she could have store-bought bread or some of the other types of food that the children brought to school. But she had never thought about helping herself to it. Not once. That would be stealing.

Teacher Rhoda looked at Lily quietly for a few minutes. It felt like an hour. Finally she said, "We'll get to the bottom of this. For now, go on outside and play."

Lily went outside, but she didn't feel like joining in the game the others were playing. Effie Kauffman spotted Lily standing by the door of the schoolhouse. "Lily got a spanking. Lily got a spanking," she chanted.

"I did not!" Lily said.

"You should have," Effie said. "Teacher Rhoda should always spank thieves."

"I am not a thief!" Lily said, eyes burning.

"Lily is a thief! Lily is a thief!" Effie chanted.

Teacher Rhoda rang the bell and Lily was relieved. She spun around and hurried to her desk. Recess would be awful if everyone thought she had stolen something.

For the first ten minutes after noon recess, Teacher Rhoda usually read a story. Not today. Instead, she looked at everyone and said, "Someone took Lavina's sandwich out of her lunch box and slipped it into Lily's. Then they took Lily's sandwich and put it in Lavina's. I expect whoever did such a thing to admit to it."

The children turned to look at Lily. Even Joseph. She wanted to disappear. Why didn't anyone believe her?

After a very long time of utter silence, Teacher Rhoda said, "Seventh grade history class." Lily was relieved to hear the shuffle of books as the classroom resumed to normal noise. She took her books out of her desk and worked on her assignments.

Just before school was over for the day, Teacher Rhoda dropped a stapled note on Lily's desk and told her to take it home to her parents. Lily quickly slipped it into her pocket. She hoped no one, especially Effie, had seen it. Only trouble-makers were given notes to take home to their parents. Aaron Yoder got them on a regular basis.

As soon as Lily walked into the kitchen, she handed Teacher Rhoda's note to Mama. A serious look came over Mama's face. She went down to the shop to talk to Papa.

When it was time to get ready for bed, Papa said that he and Mama wanted to talk to Lily. Joseph and Dannie, all ears, sat on the sofa until Papa shooed them to bed.

Lily ran the hem of her apron through her fingers while she waited for Mama to tuck Paul into bed. Papa and Mama sat on the sofa, sad looks on their kind faces. Lily felt like shouting, "But I didn't do it!" Instead, she waited quietly to hear what they had to say.

"Explain to us how you happened to end up with Lavina's sandwich in your lunch box today," Papa said.

"I don't know," Lily said. "It was in my lunch box and I thought it was mine. And my sandwich was in her lunch box."

"Those sandwiches didn't change places by themselves," Papa said.

A tear trickled down Lily's cheek. Papa and Mama didn't seem to believe her. It wasn't fair!

"Don't cry, Lily," Mama said, wiping away her tear. "Just make sure it doesn't happen again."

But that was the problem! How could Lily make sure it didn't happen again when she didn't know how it happened in the first place?

Papa's Woodwork Shop

For days now, Lily had watched Papa bring home all kinds of woodworking machinery and put it into the new basement. In the evenings he would hurry through his chores so that he could connect pipes to the machinery. Papa explained that he would buy a big diesel engine to pump hydraulic oil through the pipes. "That will make the little hydraulic motors run that are fastened to the machinery. Then I'll use air to run the small machinery like the drill press and jointer."

Lily couldn't understand any of it. Joseph, though, listened carefully to Papa's every word. Dannie pretended to understand, but Lily knew he was only trying to seem as big as Joseph. Lily would rather learn about cooking and baking than how machinery worked.

The day finally came when all the machinery was ready and Papa's shop was finished. Everyone gathered around Papa as he clamped a piece of wood into the lathe. He pulled the lever and the lathe sprang into action. The wood started spinning so fast that Lily could hardly see it. She held her hands over her ears. This was noisy!

Papa selected a wood chisel and held it against the spinning wood. Sawdust sprayed over his arms as he drew the chisel back and forth until he was satisfied with what he had made. He turned the lever off. Everything seemed peacefully quiet except for the hum of the big diesel engine outside.

Papa removed the piece of wood and handed it to Mama. "Well, what do you think, Rachel?"

"Why, it's beautiful," Mama said as she stroked her fingers over it. She handed it to Lily.

Lily looked at it closely. It really was beautiful. The ugly piece of wood that Papa had put into the lathe was now smooth and round and looked as if it had three little beads.

"The first spindle for our first chair," Papa said. He picked up another piece of wood. "I'll need a lot more of these to have enough to make a set of dining room chairs."

Mama and Lily went back upstairs to bake some cookies. They could hear the lathe going in the basement and knew Papa was making more spindles.

Lily and Joseph came home from school one afternoon to discover something new in the pine trees behind the house. Papa was setting up two used fuel tanks that he had bought from a neighbor. By his side was Dannie, acting like Papa's chief assistant. Papa stopped what he was doing when he saw Lily and Joseph. "We'll fill one with diesel fuel for the engine that runs the shop, and the other one we'll fill with gas for the garden tiller and lawn mower." He stepped back to look at them. "They sure do look ugly right now though."

Lily agreed with Papa. They sure did look ugly. The red paint was peeling off and they were covered with little rust spots.

"The next time I go to town I'll have to buy some paint and then you children can paint them for me."

Joseph and Dannie jumped up and down, hooting and hollering like they had won a prize. They were excited to paint for Papa. Lily was just as excited but lately she had been trying to practice mature and ladylike behavior. She didn't jump even though she dearly wanted to. She thought boys were born lucky. They could do whatever they wanted to and never had to worry about someone like Ida Kauffman frowning and whispering, "That's not ladylike."

On Saturday, Papa returned from a trip to town with a gallon of silver paint. He pried open the paint can lid and stirred it to make sure it was mixed properly. Satisfied, he handed paintbrushes to Lily, Joseph, and Dannie.

Lily dipped her brush into the paint and carefully stroked it on the tank. Now the tank was three colors. Ugly red, rusty orange, and beautiful shiny silver.

This was fun. The more they painted, the prettier the fuel tanks looked. After finishing one side, they picked up the paint can and went to paint the other side. After that side was done, Lily realized they had a problem. They should have painted the top first.

She dipped her paintbrush into the paint and stood on

her tiptoes to try to reach the top. She stretched as far as she could. She managed to slap her paintbrush against the top but she couldn't swish it back and forth. Then she lost her balance and fell against the tank. Her dress was covered with silver paint and so were her hands.

How awful! Joseph and Dannie laughed when they saw her dress. She could feel a few tears welling up in her eyes and tried to wipe them away. That made them laugh all the harder. "Now you have paint under your eyes, too," Joseph yelped. "Like a raccoon!"

"Like a skunk!" Dannie added.

Disgusted with them, Lily rested her paintbrush on top of the pail of paint and went into the shop to find Papa. He would know what to do.

Papa took one look at her. "What happened to you?"

"I was trying to reach the top of the fuel tank to paint it, and I fell against it," Lily said.

"Let's go wash your hands and face," Papa said. "Then you can keep painting. Don't worry about painting the top of the tanks. I should have told you that I would do it after you're done with the sides."

After washing up, Lily went back outside and helped Joseph and Dannie paint the other tank. She was relieved she didn't have to worry about painting the tops. Painting sides was much more fun.

Papa came outside and finished painting the tops for them. That evening, after the paint had dried, he took a little brush and a small can of black paint and carefully wrote GAS in big black letters on the front.

"Now we won't have to worry about getting the gas and diesel mixed up." He glanced at Joseph and Dannie. "I don't want any of you to ever open the valves on the tanks. Not ever."

Lily thought Papa was very wise to add that warning. Little boys were much too curious. But she did wish Papa had remembered to tell her that he would paint the top of the tanks. Her favorite work dress was ruined.

Joseph's Campfire Birthday

*M*ama sat at the kitchen table with a notepad and pen, scribbling down something. Lily tried to read her notes, upside down. "Joseph will be having his eighth birthday next week," she explained. "I thought we could build a nice campfire and roast hot dogs and toast some marshmallows. Maybe invite all the relatives."

What a wonderful idea! A campfire would be just the thing for a boy like Joseph. And it would be even more fun for Lily to have Cousin Hannah there. They could sit next to each other and talk while the boys did whatever boys tended to do.

Mama wrote several notes and sent Lily to deliver them. Each family said yes right away, so Lily was able to bring answers home to Mama.

When Joseph heard about the campfire birthday, he was

so happy he couldn't sit still. He decided to get right to work cleaning up some fallen tree limbs in the yard—something Papa had been meaning to do for a while now. Joseph dragged the branches and made a big pile of them in the barnyard. He was the hardest-working boy in the world. Lily couldn't help but admire the big pile of wood he had gathered. As big as a bonfire! It would make a fine campfire.

Joseph's birthday finally arrived. Lily helped Mama frost Joseph's birthday cake. She watched Mama decorate it: a little log cabin was surrounded by several pine trees and a little creek that ran through the trees. It was beautiful. She couldn't wait until Joseph saw it, but it was to be a surprise until later tonight. One thing Lily knew—Joseph would be pleased with Mama's decoration.

Mama asked Lily to find old blankets they used for picnics and to take them outside under a tree. Papa and the boys were starting the campfire. It needed to burn down to have plenty of red embers for roasting hot dogs and toasting marshmallows. Lily looked forward to eating hot dogs—they were a special, once-in-a-while treat. But most of all, she was excited to eat the toasted marshmallows. Those were the best. The very best treat of all.

After everyone arrived, the men started to sharpen sticks to roast the hot dogs. Mama and Aunt Mary scurried around to make sure everyone had a glass of lemonade or water and plenty of hot dogs to roast.

Aunt Susie sat next to Lily and Hannah. They had each eaten one hot dog and were ready to toast marshmallows. Papa had given them each a sharpened stick and showed them how to toast to perfection. One after another after another. Lily was sorry when Mama said they had eaten

enough. She would have liked to toast and eat marshmallows all night long.

Papa had gone inside and came back out with several brown paper bags. "It's time for Joseph's presents." He handed the bags to Joseph.

Everyone quieted to watch Joseph pull gifts out of the paper bags. First, he drew out a new shirt and pair of trousers. Next, a shiny new slingshot. Grandpa gave him a book filled with patterns to make birdhouses. "Now that your papa has a woodworking shop, I knew it wouldn't be long before you want to start building things, too," Grandpa said. "This should give you something easy to start out with."

Uncle Elmer's family gave him a baseball and bat. Uncle Jacob's family gave him a crisp, new five-dollar bill. Joseph thanked each family, one by one, and then it was time for everyone to go home. Lily sighed happily as she helped Mama clean up. Birthdays were a lot of fun even when they weren't hers.

Trouble Is Brewing

After the horrible day when Lily ate Lavina's sandwich, Lily checked her lunch carefully before she started to school. She wanted to be sure she knew exactly what was in it before she left for school.

During lunch, Lily was happy to see that her sandwich looked just the same as it had that morning. The mysterious sandwich switch was soon forgotten.

But something else had been switched. Lily's apple slices were missing. In her lunch box were several store-bought cookies. This time, Lily was wiser. She didn't eat a single cookie, though she loved store-bought cookies and this kind was her favorite. Malinda's head popped up and she looked around the room. "Someone took my cookies and left these apple slices."

Lily quickly gave the cookies to Malinda and took her own apple slices back to her desk.

Teacher Rhoda saw the exchange. "Who is taking food out of lunch boxes again?" Nobody answered her.

"I'm sure it was Lily," Effie said. "Her family is poor. She never has good food and always wants to eat other children's food."

Lily felt her face grow warm. It was true. Lily and Joseph rarely had store-bought treats in their lunches. And she did wish her friends would share their treats with her. But she had never, ever thought of stealing anyone's lunch.

"Did you take the cookies, Lily?" Teacher Rhoda asked in a sad voice.

"No, I didn't," Lily said. Her voice sounded wobbly. Her cheeks were burning. She was sure everyone would think she looked and sounded guilty. And she wasn't!

Teacher Rhoda's chin was firm, but her eyes were far from certain. When Lily put her lunch box on the shelf, Teacher Rhoda stopped her before she ran out the door. "Do you have any idea how those cookies got into your lunch box? Any idea at all?"

"No, I don't," Lily said.

"Lily, you must know that lying is almost as bad as stealing."

"But I'm not lying," Lily said. Why didn't Teacher Rhoda believe her?

"Why would someone else exchange food in your lunch box?"

"I don't know," Lily said miserably.

Teacher Rhoda didn't seem to know what to say. "Try to make sure it doesn't happen again."

But how?! Lily wanted to ask. She went outside but recess had been spoiled for her. The entire day had been spoiled for her. How awful that no one believed she was telling the truth! She almost always told the truth.

At suppertime, Lily didn't want to eat very much. When Papa asked her what was wrong, she told him how someone had put Malinda's cookies into her lunch box and her apple slices into Malinda's lunch box.

Papa and Mama exchanged a look. A very worried look.

Weeks passed. Three more times, someone else's food turned up in Lily's lunch box. It was always store-bought food and always from a different child's lunch. Teacher Rhoda asked each student if he or she knew who was exchanging the food. No one knew. If they knew, they weren't telling. Lily was sure they were all blaming her. Even Cousin Hannah and Beth, her best friends, had started to treat her differently. They didn't always include her in recess games or ask her to sit with them or share secrets with her. More and more, Lily sat alone and read books during lunch and recess.

School was no longer a fun place to be. Lily wished she could just stay home.

Marshmallow Mess

After breakfast one Saturday, Mama told Lily that she was going to town with Aunt Mary. "I'll take baby Paul with me," Mama said. "Hannah, Levi, and Davy will stay here until we come back. I'm sure Levi and Joseph will be fine, but you and Hannah should keep an eye on Dannie and Davy. You can have all day to play. Papa will be in the shop, if you need anything."

Lily was nervous, but excited. Hannah hadn't come over to play in weeks. At school, Hannah acted a little stiff and uncomfortable around Lily—as if she just wasn't sure if Lily was or wasn't a sandwich thief. Maybe a whole day to play together, without anyone else around from school, would set things right between them.

Aunt Mary drove the buggy up to the house and waited while her children climbed out and Mama and baby Paul climbed in. "Be good, and have fun," Aunt Mary and Mama said at the exact same time. Lily thought it was funny that they were so much alike. They looked alike, they sounded alike, they even talked alike. Why couldn't Lily have a sister? It seemed like so much fun.

Hannah had run alongside the buggy to wave goodbye to her mother, then she turned and walked up to join Lily on the porch. In the quiet, things grew awkward again. "What do you want to do today?" Hannah asked.

"Anything you'd like to do," Lily said. She wanted Hannah to have a good time.

Hannah tilted her head, as if something was whirling in her mind. Lily grinned. She knew Hannah was thinking up something fun and interesting. A little dangerous, but not too dangerous. Hannah had good ideas.

"Hmmm . . . I wish," Hannah started, tapping her chin, "I wish we could have another campfire like we had for Joseph's birthday."

Lily's gaze shifted to the kitchen window. "We still have a whole bag of marshmallows left over."

"Let's toast them!" Hannah said.

Lily rolled that over in her mind. Too risky. "We can't make a campfire."

"Maybe we can come up with a solution . . . if we think hard enough."

A wonderful idea popped into Lily's head. "I have just the thing! We could light the kitchen oil lamp and put a marshmallow on a fork and hold it above the chimney to toast it."

"Great idea!" Hannah said as they both ran to the house.

In the kitchen, Lily carefully removed the glass chimney of the oil lamp. She struck a match and lit the wick, then replaced the chimney and adjusted the wick until it was burning just right: a nice flame but no smoke.

She ran into the pantry to fetch the bag of marshmallows while Hannah found forks in a kitchen drawer. She let Hannah toast the first marshmallow. It took a long time until she was satisfied that it was a golden brown. Hannah popped it into her mouth. "Perfect!" she said, opening a mouthful of chewy marshmallow.

Now it was Lily's turn. She held the fork with the marshmallow above the chimney. She kept turning it to make sure the marshmallow would toast nicely on all sides. This was taking so long. The marshmallow wasn't even turning a color yet. She was hungry for a toasted marshmallow right now! If she could only get the marshmallow closer to the heat, then it could toast on all sides.

Holding the fork, she poked the marshmallow down inside the chimney. It didn't take long at all before the marshmallow was beautifully golden brown and puffy. As Lily tried to pull it back out, it got stuck against the sides of the chimney. She pulled a little harder. Her fork flew out but the marshmallow stayed stuck. Then it turned black. Lily tried to blow the flame out, but the marshmallow was blocking it. A horrible smell filled the air. Hannah screamed.

Think quick, Lily! She ran to get a pot holder. Then she removed the chimney and blew out the flame. Problem solved! She carried the chimney over to the sink to clean out the sticky marshmallow that was stuck inside. She opened the faucet and let water run over it. There was a loud cracking noise and the chimney broke into pieces.

Hannah and Lily stared at the mess. How would she explain this to Mama? She and Hannah were supposed to keep an eye on Dannie and Davy. Mama assumed those little boys were the ones who might get into trouble. Instead, it was Lily.

"Let's hide it," Hannah whispered. She found a paper bag in the pantry and started to pluck pieces of glass from the kitchen sink and drop them into the bag.

"But where?" Lily said. "Dannie finds everything." She picked up a shard of sticky, marshmallowy broken glass.

Hannah's eyebrows knit together in a frown. "Where is a place Dannie wouldn't go exploring?"

Lily rinsed the last slivers of broken glass down the drain, reviewing her hiding places in her mind. Her bedroom was out. Dannie often poked around in her room while she was in school. She thought of hiding the paper bag in the basement, but he would find it while he was supposed to be helping Mama with the laundry. Papa's workshop wouldn't work. Then her face broke into a smile. "My old attic bedroom! No one goes up there."

The girls took the stairs two at a time, threw open the red door, and went up the last stairwell, a little out of breath. Lily opened the attic door and peeked her head in. She wanted to be sure no bats were swooshing around. She took a few steps inside and turned in a circle, gazing at her lovely room with the purple painted floor. She hadn't realized how much she missed it—the little window at the far end where she could see over the tops of trees. The quiet—so quiet! No sounds of little brothers galloping by.

Hannah was hunting for a place to hide the broken chimney. The room was mostly empty, except for a few pieces of furniture. She spied an old dresser in the corner and opened drawers, then closed them. "Too obvious." Then she dropped to her knees and tucked the paper bag under the dresser. She pushed it far up against the wall, jumped to her feet, stepped back to look at it carefully, then patted her palms together as if she were dusting flour from her hands. "I think we found the perfect spot. No one would ever think to look here."

"But what do we do about replacing the chimney?" Lily asked. She wasn't as quick a thinker as Hannah about these types of things.

Hannah bit her lip, thinking hard. "You can use the chimney from the lamp in your room. Then, next time you go to town, you'll have to buy a new one at the hardware store and sneak it home."

That sounded expensive. How much did a glass chimney cost, anyway? She had only two dollars and fifty-three cents left in her piggy bank. And how would she read at night without her oil lamp? It also sounded like a plan in which, very likely, she would get caught. But then they heard Jim's familiar clip-clop as he turned the buggy into the driveway and they didn't have time for more brainstorming. Mama was home.

The girls hurried back down the stairs before Jim reached the barn. On the second floor, Hannah grabbed the chimney from the lamp in Lily's room. In the kitchen, she placed it on the oil lamp on the kitchen table. Lily glanced around the kitchen, making sure all traces of marshmallow were gone and everything looked normal.

Then she had a happy thought. Today, everything *was* normal. Being with Hannah felt easy and natural again! The strain of the sandwich switch was over. Lily smiled. Life was good again.

Aaron Yoder Surprises Lily

*I*t was funny, Lily thought as she turned off her oil lamp and climbed into bed on Wednesday evening, how something as silly as a marshmallow could heal a friendship. On Monday and Tuesday of that week, Hannah and Lily had acted like they always did—they sat together at lunch, they played games at recess, they walked home together behind Joseph and Levi. With Hannah acting friendly toward Lily at school, the other girls did too. Even Effie.

Today, Hannah had brought a surprise for her. She'd waited until Joseph and Levi had run past the bend in the road and were out of sight, then opened up her lunch box and handed Lily a paper bag. Inside was a new glass chimney! "We had a lot of extras in the basement," Hannah said.

Lily tucked the paper bag in her lunch box. When she arrived home, Mama was upstairs with baby Paul so she was able to tiptoe to her room and slip the substitute chimney

68

back on her bedroom lamp. No lies were told and none were needed. But sneaking around took a toll on Lily. She had let out a big sigh of relief when the new chimney was in place and the story was over.

Later that night, Lily snuggled down deep in the covers and pulled them up under her chin. The weather was getting colder at night and in the morning. As she drifted off to sleep, she thought about how she had a new appreciation for marshmallows.

On Thursday morning, during first recess, Lily ran into the schoolhouse to put on her sweater. As she pulled it off the hook, the row of lunch boxes caught her eye. She decided to check her lunch box to make sure there was nothing in it that didn't belong there. She had helped Mama make an egg sandwich this very morning. But inside her lunch was a sandwich of store-bought bread and deli meat! She pulled it out. She wanted to switch it back and get her own sandwich. But which lunch box had her sandwich in it?

She opened one and looked inside. It wasn't there. She checked the next lunch box. Still no egg sandwich on Mama's wheat bread. She got several lunch boxes off the shelf and knelt on the floor beside them. She opened one. Nothing. She opened the next and breathed a sigh of relief. There it was! The egg salad sandwich. She quickly got it out and put the one that didn't belong to her into the lunch box. She closed it but before she could put all the lunch boxes back on the shelf, the schoolhouse door opened. There stood Teacher Rhoda, hands on her hips, a shocked look on her pretty face.

"Oh Lily," she said in an unfamiliar voice. "I had so wanted to believe you when you said you didn't know how those things got into your lunch box."

Lily scrambled to her feet. "I wasn't getting someone else's lunch! I checked on my lunch box and there was someone else's sandwich. I was trying to put the lunches back the way they belonged."

Clearly, Teacher Rhoda didn't believe her. "Put the lunch boxes back on the shelf. Then I want you to go sit at your desk."

Lily put the lunch boxes back on the shelf and walked to her desk. This couldn't be happening! Her stomach felt all tied up in knots. She was afraid she was going to be sick.

Teacher Rhoda brought several pieces of paper over to Lily. "You will be staying in at recess until you have written 'Thou shalt not steal' and 'Thou shalt not covet' one thousand times."

Lily started to cry. She couldn't help it. It simply wasn't fair. She counted the lines on one piece of paper. Twenty-five. That meant she had to write forty pages. She wasn't going to get to play outside for a long, long time. She would be a withered old lady by the time she could go back out for recess. Through the open window, she heard her friends play a hand-clapping game out in the yard, their laughter bright as sleigh bells.

Teacher Rhoda sent another note home from school for Papa and Mama. It made Lily start to cry again.

At home, Lily showed Mama and Papa the note from Teacher Rhoda. She explained what had happened that day, trying not to cry. Then she waited and waited while Papa and Mama had a private talk in their bedroom. Lily heard the low buzz of their murmuring, and Joseph offered to stick a

glass against the wall to eavesdrop, but Lily said no. She was in enough trouble.

What if Mama and Papa didn't believe her? She might have to run away and live with Grandma Miller.

"But of course we believe you," Papa said when he and Mama returned to the kitchen. "We know our little girl, and we know you wouldn't do something like that."

Lily was so relieved!

"But—"

Lily's heart sank. Anytime a sentence started with *but*, it wasn't good news.

"—we still want you to write those lines for Teacher Rhoda," Papa said. "She thinks you are guilty. It doesn't hurt to dwell on the Ten Commandments. It will certainly help you to never be tempted to take something that doesn't belong to you."

Joseph offered to help Lily, but his handwriting was awful. It was a sweet offer, though. Lily's hand cramped by the time the last line had been written. She never wanted to write such lines again. Not ever.

Two days later, Lily sat at her desk to eat her lunch. She found a small bag of potato chips inside and knew that Mama hadn't packed them. This time, Lily wasn't going to wait for someone to accuse her. She lifted up the bag for everyone to see. "Someone put potato chips into my lunch box," she said. "My apple slices are missing."

Lavina looked up, shocked. "They're mine! Here are your apples."

Lily traded with her and went back to her desk.

Aaron Yoder raised his hand. "I know how those chips got into Lily's lunch box."

Lily's head whipped around to face Aaron. "How?" Teacher Rhoda and Lily asked at the exact same time.

Aaron looked at Effie. "I saw Effie do it in first recess."

Lily didn't know whether to be suspicious about what Aaron said or amazed that he was sticking up for her.

"Effie, what do you have to say about that?" Teacher Rhoda asked.

Instantly, an expression of great boredom fell over Effie's face. Lily thought she might yawn.

That only made Teacher Rhoda angry. "Effie, you will

stay in after everyone else is done eating. And I think we all owe Lily an apology for blaming her for stealing lunches."

It was the best recess of Lily's life. Naturally, she didn't gloat. But she was quite satisfied with how things had turned out. Shocked that Aaron Yoder had done her a good turn. She felt light and happy and giggly, even though her hand still hurt from writing all those lines. She hoped that Teacher Rhoda would make Effie write thousands and thousands of lines. Maybe even a million.

Lily Bones

$\mathcal{L}$ily stretched her toes to touch the last few leaves left on the branch above her as Joseph pushed the swing as hard as he could. Autumn was under way and soon it would be too cold to swing. They loved to play on the swing Papa had made in the big tree in front of the house. It was fun to sail through the air. Lily felt light and happy all over.

Joseph stood to the side of the swing. "It's my turn now." When the swing slowed down, Lily hopped off. Joseph climbed on the swing and Lily started pushing him—higher and higher, faster and faster. They were having a contest to see who could touch the last red leaf clinging to a branch. As soon as Lily realized Joseph was about to reach it, she stopped pushing. He was close to touching it only because she was a much better swing pusher than he was. Joseph would just have to pump his legs harder.

Something caught her eye. The curtain in the attic window ruffled in the breeze.

She decided to take Sally, her doll, and a book up to the room to play. "I'm tired of swinging," she said. She ran to the house.

"Hey!" Joseph yelled. "Not fair! Come back! I still need a few more pushes."

Lily ran back and gave him a few more pushes. Then she went to the house and found her doll and book. She ran up the stairs and into the little attic bedroom. Her gaze swept the empty room and she sighed. It was so lovely. Even without her furniture and purple rag rug.

Lily changed her doll's dress and rocked her to sleep. She lay Sally carefully on a blanket and swaddled her, the way she had seen Mama swaddle baby Paul when he was a newborn. But playing with Sally wasn't as much fun as it used to be. Sally had become a little dull.

Her tummy growled. She thought she might go back down to the kitchen and get a snack when she remembered the glass chimney covered with gooey marshmallows that she had hidden underneath a dresser. It had been only a week. If she were very, very careful, maybe she could scrape some leftover marshmallow off a large piece and eat it for a snack!

She crouched down on her knees and put a hand under the dresser. She felt cobwebs and dust, then her hand touched the paper bag that held the chimney pieces. She pulled it out from under the dresser and opened the bag—then gagged. What had happened to the marshmallow? There was fuzzy, grayish-green mold covering the chimney. It smelled horrible. She tucked it back under the dresser, as far as it would go, and decided she wasn't hungry after all.

Lily picked up her book and soon was lost in the story. A couple of flies buzzed through the open window and circled around her. There was nothing quite so annoying as a fly buzzing around your head when you were trying to read. Though, Lily thought, having a mosquito buzz around your head when you were trying to sleep was equally annoying. She closed the window firmly and heard a thump and rattle outside the door. She paused to listen, but didn't hear anything more, so she went back to her book.

The next thing Lily knew, she heard a little fluttering sound. A familiar, horrible fluttering sound. Something whirred past her face. She shrieked and ducked, covered her head with her arms, then opened one eye carefully to peep under her elbow. A bat! She shielded her head with her book and ran to the door. The handle turned but the door didn't open. She tried again but it still didn't move an inch. She used her shoulder to push on the door as hard as she could, but it was no use. The door was stuck.

Lily felt a spike of worry. Hunger, too. The sun was starting to lay low in the sky. She had stayed in the attic room much longer than she had planned to. Why hadn't Mama called her to come help with supper? Then it dawned on her—no one knew where she had gone. She hadn't told Joseph. Maybe Mama did call for her and Lily hadn't heard her.

Lily started to panic. What if no one ever found her? What if she starved to death up in this attic? The bat flew past again, swooping and dipping. How had it gotten into this room? From the corner of her eye, she saw something dark slip through the attic duct, then unfold its wings and dart across the ceiling. Another bat!

Tears started streaming down Lily's face as she pounded

on the door and called for help. She became hot and sweaty from pounding. Her throat grew hoarse from shouting. She slipped down against the door and sat on the floor, worn out from pounding and calling. Oh this was terrible. Just terrible! She was going to die. She was going to die in this stuffy, bat-infested attic. Someday, Mama and Papa would go to the attic and find a pile of bones. Lily bones.

She sank into a ball by the door, trying to make herself as small as possible. She covered her head with her apron, but then wasn't sure if it would be better to actually see the bats flying around again and know for certain where they were, or not to see them and wonder. She alternated between peeking at the bats and hiding from them. Now there were three bats—swooping, whirring, diving, and darting as if they were having the time of their lives. Soon, she was sure, there would be hundreds. They probably held bat parties each night in her beautiful attic bedroom.

She tried not to cry again. She didn't want to cry. But she was scared and worried and one tear started, then another and another. She wiped her eyes with the apron and noticed that the sky had grown even darker. The first evening star twinkled at her through the little window.

The window.

The window! Why hadn't Lily thought of the window? She ran across the room and opened it. The cool evening air felt as good and refreshing as a drink of water. She stuck her head outside the window. "Help!" she shouted, as loudly as she could.

Far below, near the barn, Papa froze when he heard her voice call out. "Lily! Lily!" Papa yelled, turning in a circle to locate her. "Lily, where are you? Mama and I have been looking everywhere for you!"

Lily waved and waved. "I'm here, Papa! Up here!"

Papa looked up toward the attic and saw her. "What are you doing up there?"

"I can't get out!" She cupped her hands. "AND THERE ARE BATS IN HERE!"

"I'm coming!" Papa bolted up to the house.

Lily was so relieved. She wouldn't end up as a pile of bones, after all. She closed the window and hurried to the door to wait for Papa.

Lily could hear Papa doing something on the other side of the door. Then the handle turned and the door opened and there stood Papa. Lily ran into his arms. "My, you gave us a scare," Papa said. "We didn't know where you were."

"I called and called but nobody heard me."

"Some boxes tumbled down in front of the door. I hadn't re-alized this house was so well insulated that the sound wouldn't carry. The next time you want to come up here to play, let Mama know where you are. Just in case boxes tumble down again."

"Papa, I found out how the bats are getting in!" She pointed to the attic duct.

Papa peered at the duct, then moved the dresser and climbed up on it to get a closer look. Lily held her breath when she saw the paper bag, exposed. A bat slipped in through the duct and whizzed by his head. He jumped off the dresser and pushed it back in place. Lily exhaled. "I'll deal with this later," he said. "For now, let's go tell Mama you're safe and sound."

Lily followed Papa down to the kitchen. Mama was wait-ing at the bottom of the stairs, relieved to see her. Joseph and Dannie were at their places at the kitchen table, waiting impatiently for her. Even baby Paul waved his spoon at her, eager to eat. She forgave them, though. They were just little boys. They couldn't be expected to understand that she had narrowly escaped death.

As Lily sat at the table, she felt so content. She was the luckiest girl in the world. She had barely survived a harrowing ordeal. She had a Papa and a Mama who were searching for her. And she had three brothers who loved her enough to not eat, even though they wanted to, until they knew she was safe and sound.

"One good thing about Lily's adventure," Papa said, eyes smiling. "She found out how the bats are getting in."

Joseph and Dannie were all ears and eyes. They even stopped eating to hear the answer to the bat mystery.

"Attic ducts have screens on them," Papa said. "At least, they're supposed to. But one of them doesn't have a screen. I didn't even notice that when I installed it. That's how the bats had been getting in." He lathered a biscuit with butter. "I'll get a screen on that tomorrow morning."

Mama passed Lily a bowl of green peas. "Lily, would you want to move back up to the attic after Papa fixes the screen?"

Lily took her time answering, scooping peas onto her plate. The attic bedroom was very special, but it had some serious drawbacks. She felt far away from the family, and what if she got locked in again? Next time, she might not be discovered until it was too late. Till she was just a pile of Lily bones. "I think," she said, chewing her peas, "I think I'll just stay where I am."

Besides, there was the disgusting marshmallow chimney to consider.

CHAPTER

14

Papa's Surprise

*N*ot fair. It just wasn't fair to be a girl sometimes.

Joseph and Dannie clambered up over the front wheel of the spring wagon to sit next to Papa on the wagon seat. Papa slapped the reins and Jim proudly trotted down the driveway, away down the road. Lily sighed. She watched from the kitchen window and felt terribly sorry for herself.

Papa was taking the boys to an estate auction. Lily loved auctions. They were fascinating! All kinds of strange things would be sold. She liked to listen to the fast-paced chant of the auctioneer as he encouraged people to bid higher for the items. How could anyone understand him? Best of all was that Papa let her choose something to eat from the food stand. She had so wanted to go today, but Mama needed her to stay at home to help with Saturday cleaning and to keep baby Paul out of trouble.

It just wasn't fair to be a girl. She was Lily, the oldest child, she reminded herself. But today she left like Lily, the only child.

There was one good thing about the day, but just one. And it wasn't a very *big* good thing. It was a little good thing. With Joseph and Dannie gone, it took Mama and Lily half the normal time to finish their regular cleaning. Usually, those brothers ran in and out of the house, interrupting Mama, annoying Lily, tracking dirt on the sparkling clean floors. Baby Paul, still a baby and not a full-fledged boy yet, happily played with his toy animals and wooden blocks all morning. Mama and Lily were done in no time at all.

Mama finished mopping the floor. She rested her chin on top of the mop pole. "Lily, today would be a fine day to wax the kitchen floor. With Papa and the boys gone, we don't have to worry about them tracking in dirt on the floor before the wax has time to dry."

She seemed pleased. Lily was not pleased. She had hoped they might bake cookies. Or make candy.

"Paul is still playing happily," Mama said, ignoring Lily's lack of enthusiasm. "If we hurry, he should be fine until we get done."

Mama plucked the big jug of wax off the shelf in the broom closet and handed several small rags to Lily. She showed Lily how to pour a stream of wax on the floor and carefully spread it evenly over every inch.

In a way, it was a little bit like icing a cupcake. A very, very big cupcake. Every swish of the rag made the floor look new and shiny. Mama let Lily pour another stream of wax on the floor and swish her rag back and forth through it. Lily was nearly having fun, if you could find anything fun about cleaning a house. Nearly. But she didn't like that her fingers stuck together, just as if she had glued them. And the wax was stinky, too.

Lily backed up to see how shiny the floor was looking. She

didn't realize the jug was right behind her. Her heel knocked it over and a big puddle of wax spilled all over the floor. Lily grabbed the jug and Mama hurried to get more rags. At that exact moment, baby Paul toddled into the kitchen. "Milk!" Lily heard him say, right before he stepped into the puddle of wax and his feet flew out from under him. He plopped right down in the middle of it and Lily expected him to start howling—but he was distracted by the wax puddle. He started swishing his hands and was quickly covered with stinky, sticky wax.

Mama came back into the kitchen with the rags. Her eyes went wide and her mouth opened in a big O. She dropped the rags and picked Paul up. "I think it's time for you to have a bath, clean clothes, and a nice, long nap. In that order."

At the foot of the stairs, she stopped and turned, hesitation on her face. "Lily, do you think you can finish the floor while I take care of Paul?"

"Oh, yes!" How fun! "I'll be extra careful not to spill any more wax," Lily said. "Don't you worry about a thing, Mama. Not a thing."

Mama seemed a little worried. "Take your time and go slow. Then, after you're done, you can have the rest of the day to play."

That sounded like an ideal arrangement. Lily could keep icing the cupcake floor and she didn't have a single brother around to bother her. Not one. And then she could play.

Carefully, oh so carefully, Lily finished waxing the rest of the floor. She tried not to spill a drop. She couldn't wait to put away the jug of wax and wash her hands. Lily thought about leaving the wax on her nails. It made them look pretty and shiny, but her hands felt sticky and smelled bad. She decided to go ahead and wash them. That jug of wax had caused enough trouble for one day, and Lily didn't want Mama to have to tell her why she couldn't have shiny fingernails. She knew just what she would say: Too fancy.

Lily washed and washed and washed her hands, thinking about what she should do next. Playing outside wasn't as much fun without Joseph and Dannie. She went to her room to get Sally, her doll. She dressed Sally in her nicest clothes and wrapped her in the prettiest blanket. She tried to play with Sally but it wasn't fun like it used to be. She felt bored with Sally.

Lily put the doll away and went to see what Mama was up to. She found her in the living room, sitting on her rocking chair, knitting a pair of bedroom slippers. She put down her knitting needles when Lily came into the room. "Don't you know what to do?"

"No," Lily said. "I tried to play with Sally, but it wasn't any fun." She sighed. "Sally's changed."

Mama smiled, but it seemed like a sad smile. "You're growing up, Lily. The things that used to be fun for you haven't changed, but you are growing past them."

Lily pondered that comment. It made her feel good and bad, all at the same time. She was glad Mama realized she was growing up, but it made her feel sad that she was getting too old to have fun playing with Sally.

Mama picked up her needles and started to knit again. Her fingers flew. "Do you want me to teach you how to knit?" Mama said. "You could start with a nice scarf."

Oh no! Knitting looked even worse than sewing something by hand.

"Maybe another day," Lily said. "I'll find something else to do." Anything else. Except cleaning, sewing, and washing dishes.

Lily heard Papa's voice talking to Jim. "Whoa. Back up. Easy boy. Whoa." She dropped her book on the bed and ran to the window. Papa was backing Jim and the spring wagon up to the garage door in front of the shop. The spring wagon was piled high. She couldn't wait to see what kinds of treasures Papa had brought home from the auction. She flew outside to investigate.

Papa grinned when he saw the excitement on Lily's face. "Go ask Mama if she can come help me unload some of these things."

Lily ran back to the house to tell Mama that Papa needed her. Mama tucked her knitting needles into the ball of yarn, put whatever she was knitting into her basket, and got up from her rocking chair. "Lily, I need you to stay inside so you can hear Paul when he wakes up from his nap."

Lily froze, horrified. She had wanted to run outside to see all the things Papa had bought as he unloaded them off the wagon. This was just one more reason why it wasn't fair to be a girl and to be the oldest. Joseph was never asked to wait inside for baby Paul to wake up. It wasn't just because Joseph wouldn't have remembered to listen for baby Paul, even though that would have been true. It was because he was a boy. And he was thought to be too little to do anything except have fun. She cracked open a window and heard the excited voices of Joseph and Dannie as they explained their purchases to Mama.

Not fair. So not fair.

She wanted baby Paul to wake up right now so she could take him outside. She crept into the bedroom to see if he was still sleeping.

His eyes were closed, his arms were above his head, and his favorite little teddy bear was tucked beside him, under the blanket. He looked so cute and peaceful. On any other day, Lily would have tiptoed away, hoping he wouldn't wake up for hours and hours. But today wasn't an ordinary day.

Lily coughed.

She coughed again. Louder.

She reached into his crib and lifted one of his little hands, but he kept right on sleeping. She tickled his toes, but he only wiggled his feet a little. He went right on sleeping like a bear snoozing away the winter.

Lily sighed. It wasn't fair. Everyone was having fun except her. She heard Dannie squeal with delight. Something was going on and she didn't know what.

She couldn't stand it another minute. She reached into the crib and picked Paul up. He blinked his eyes in surprise, yawned, and stretched.

The trick was to keep him happy. If he woke too early, he could be a grouch. Lily talked cheerfully to him as she walked to the kitchen. She offered him a drink of water. He took a few sips and seemed like he was starting to wake up. Lily held him on her left hip and hurried outside to see what was happening.

Mama looked puzzled when she saw Lily carrying Paul. "Is he up already?"

Lily avoided her eyes and nodded. She wasn't telling a lie. Not yet. But if Mama asked her anything else, she might admit that she had woken Paul on purpose. She felt fairly confident that Mama would not like that.

Lily looked at the treasures spread on the ground. There were several boxes filled with pretty dishes and books. Lily hoped Mama would let her sift through the boxes to see what was there. Mama was busy helping Papa lift a big desk off the back of the spring wagon. Lily wondered why Papa had bought another desk. He already had one in the living room.

When Papa had put the desk on the ground, he turned to Lily. "What do you think of this desk?"

Paul was wide awake and started to squirm. He wanted to get down and see what Dannie was doing. "I think it's nice," Lily said.

Papa's eyes twinkled. "I bought it for you. I know how much you like to read and write. I thought it would be nice if you had your very own desk in your room."

Lily looked at Papa, then at the desk, then back at Papa. Had she heard him correctly? He had a big grin on his face. How wonderful! She would have her very own desk. "Can we take it to my room right now?"

Papa laughed. "Not today. We'll have to rearrange the furniture in your bedroom to make room for it. I have to get started on the evening chores. But we'll try to get it moved in on Monday."

Monday? That was two days from now. Lily tried not to feel let down. It was hard to have something so wonderful come into your life, right in front of you . . . and then to have to wait. Life just wasn't fair.

But . . . it was more fair now than it was this morning.

Lily finished her geography assignment and put everything neatly inside her desk. She looked at the clock. There were still twenty-five minutes before school would dismiss. She watched the second hand make its round from number to number with slow, jerking moves. One minute ticked away. Only twenty-four minutes left.

Lily wished the clock would hurry up and move faster. She wanted to go home and see if Papa and Mama had moved the new desk into her bedroom already. She felt a little giddy—a Christmas morning giddy. How would her room look with the desk in it? She couldn't wait to fill the drawers with paper and books and all her scrapbook supplies. She decided to get to work again on a scrapbook for Grandpa Lapp. She had started it last year but lost interest. A new desk would make scrapbooking more fun.

Teacher Rhoda tapped the bell on her desk twice to signal that it was time for everyone to put their books away and get ready to go home. All around Lily was the noise of books closing and desk lids opening. After everyone had their things tucked neatly inside their desks, the students stood, sang the closing hymn and, finally, Lily could go. She dashed to the back of the schoolhouse, grabbed her lunch pail from the shelf, and darted out the door.

"Wait for me, Lily," Hannah called out.

Lily slowed down until Hannah caught up with her.

"What's the big hurry?"

"Papa bought a real desk just for me. I want to go home and use it."

"We do enough writing in school. Why would you want to hurry home and write some more?"

"I can do more than just write at the desk," Lily said. "I can make scrapbooks like Grandma Miller does. I can draw pictures and paint. I can do anything I want to."

Hannah didn't share Lily's enthusiasm and was in no hurry to get home. "Did you see how far Aaron Yoder batted the ball at recess today?"

Lily rolled her eyes. Hannah talked about how wonderful Aaron Yoder was all the way home from school. Every single day.

"He batted a home run."

"So did a few of the other boys. And they aren't as much of a pest as Aaron is."

Hannah ignored her. "Aaron is so smart! He gets his lessons done faster than anyone else in school. He has such excellent penmanship. Just excellent. Haven't you noticed?"

Lily wondered if Hannah might be getting slightly addled. Aaron's handwriting wasn't neat and tidy. Just the opposite! Teacher Rhoda scolded him for messy writing nearly every other day.

After the sandwich switch, Lily was so happy to spend time with Hannah again that she politely tolerated her ridiculous talk about Aaron. Plus, Aaron had done her one nice thing when he told Teacher Rhoda that Effie was the culprit. But that was the only nice thing Aaron had ever done for Lily, and now he was back to being his pesky old self. Lily couldn't stand listening to Hannah moon over Aaron Yoder. She actually felt relieved when they reached the path where Hannah turned off.

Lily burst into the house and galloped up the stairs. She didn't even stop to see if Mama had a snack waiting on the kitchen table. When she reached her bedroom door, she stopped abruptly. There it was! Her very own desk. Mama had picked a bouquet of flowers and put them in a vase on the corner of the desk. On the other corner were her oil lamp and her little apple-shaped candy dish. All the furniture in her room had been rearranged to allow room for the desk. Even the floor looked as if Mama had given it a new coat of wax.

Lily walked over to the desk and opened a few drawers. All delightfully empty—just waiting for her to put something inside.

Dannie came running into her room. "I helped Mama wax your floor. I helped pick the flowers too and fill your candy dish."

"Thank you," Lily said. She lifted the lid off of the candy dish and was pleased to see it was almost full. She would make this candy last for a long time. She would eat a piece only on Saturdays. Maybe Sundays, too. Only twice a week would she eat candy.

Dannie stood at the doorjamb, watching and smiling. Finally, Lily asked, "Is there something else I should see?"

Dannie clapped his hands. "Open the drawer. I shared some of my treasures."

Lily opened another drawer. "Oh, Dannie," she said when she saw what he had tucked inside: a pile of small stones, several pinecones, and some wood scraps from the shop.

He was so pleased! But Lily didn't want any of that junk messing up her beautiful desk. "That was kind of you, Dannie," she said. "But I know how much these treasures mean to you. Why don't you keep them for me?" She scooped them out of the drawer and handed them to him.

Somehow, Dannie seemed even more pleased.

Just as he left, baby Paul toddled into her room. Lily scooped him up into her arms. "Did you climb the stairs all by yourself?" Lily said. Paul was getting to be quite a climber. Mama said every time she turned around, he was climbing up on something.

Lily couldn't work at her new desk with Paul bothering her. She took him downstairs and helped Mama get supper ready. She plopped him on the floor beside the toy box and started building a tower with the wooden blocks. As soon as Paul became interested in the toys, she quietly got up to set the table.

After the table was set, Lily sat on a stool at the end of the kitchen counter to watch Mama cook and talk to her. This was one of Lily's favorite times of the day. She had Mama all to herself and could tell her about her day at school. Today, she admitted how frustrated she felt with Cousin Hannah. "She just doesn't see Aaron Yoder in the right light!"

"It's called wearing rose-colored glasses," Mama said. "It means you see things the way you want them to be."

That was a new phrase to Lily and it suited the situation perfectly. Hannah wore rose-colored glasses with Aaron Yoder.

"That's not all bad, Lily. Hannah is just believing the best about a person."

Just as Lily opened her mouth to explain that where Aaron Yoder was concerned, it was best to assume the worst about him, a horrible crash came from upstairs. A second later, a wailing sound floated down the stairs.

"Where is Paul?" Mama asked.

"He had been playing with his toys in the living room."

Paul's cries grew louder. Mama went upstairs and Lily followed. The door to Lily's bedroom was open and there was Paul sitting on the floor. His mouth and hands were covered with melted chocolate. Beside him was Lily's little apple dish, broken.

Mama checked Paul to make sure he wasn't hurt after tumbling off the desk. Then she took him downstairs to clean him up. Lily sat on her bed with the broken pieces of her candy dish. Tears pricked her eyes. What a disappointment. Her very first day with her new desk had not gone well.

During supper, Lily told Papa about her broken candy dish. He asked to see the pieces, so she ran upstairs to get them.

"This shouldn't be too hard to glue back together," Papa said, examining the pieces. "It's a clean break."

After dinner, Papa glued Lily's apple dish. By bedtime, it was back on her desk. It amazed her—Papa could fix anything. But from now on, she was going to keep her door shut tight. Too many nosy little brothers.

Lily, the Famous Artist

On a Saturday afternoon in October, a whiskered man drove up to Whispering Pines to talk to Papa. Last summer, Papa and Uncle Jacob had built a mini barn for that man and still hadn't been paid for the work. Lily knew that because she had overheard Papa and Mama talking about it. Now the man was telling Papa that he had lost his job and couldn't pay him. "I hoped you might accept a barter deal," the man said to Papa. "I've got some things you and your children might like."

In the back of the man's trunk was a box filled with paints, paintbrushes, and books about painting. Lily wanted Papa to take the things. They looked so much more interesting than money. There were also tools and a lawn mower. "Please take the stuff, Papa," Lily whispered under her breath. "Please take the stuff."

Papa stroked his short curly beard, a sign that he was thinking it over. He took his hat off and ran his fingers through his hair. "I hadn't been planning on buying any of these things."

The man shuffled his feet and cleared his throat. "I don't know when I can pay you." He looked embarrassed.

Lily felt sorry for him. *Take the stuff, Papa!*

Papa put his hat back on. "Let me go talk to my wife about it."

Lily blew air out of her mouth. Mama didn't like to buy things they didn't need. Like the goats. Papa had bought the goats from a man in a truck whose wife was mad at him. Mama had not been happy about those goats. They were always causing trouble.

Papa walked to the house, so Lily and Joseph went to play on the swing. Lily wanted to go inside and help Papa persuade Mama to keep all of that wonderful stuff in the man's truck. But she knew that wouldn't do. Papa and Mama liked to make these decisions without her excellent suggestions, she had been told. Once or twice.

Lily squeezed her eyes tight. *Please Mama, don't say no!* She was already imagining what she would paint with those fancy paintbrushes. She was sure if she followed the instructions in those books she would become a great artist.

Amazingly, when Papa came back outside, he had a big grin on his face. Papa and the man unloaded everything from the back of the truck.

Later that evening, as soon as the supper dishes were finished, Lily asked Mama if she could start painting.

Mama smiled. "I'll help you get started." She selected a few pieces of heavy paper and put them on the table. Lily looked at all of the paintbrushes. There were so many different sizes. How could anyone know which one to use?

Mama picked up one of the paint instruction books and flipped through it. She opened it up to a brightly colored page. "I think you could paint some roses." She sat in a chair next to Lily and helped her select the correct brush. She explained how to paint the rose.

Lily carefully followed Mama's instructions. When she finished, she held it up to admire it. It didn't look quite as pretty as the one in the instruction book but it had been fun to paint. Soon, she would be the best artist in the family. She had no doubt of that. She set to work on another rose.

Too soon, Papa called out in his deep, kind voice, "Bedtime for little lambs."

94

Lily gathered the paint supplies and put them on the back shelf of the pantry, where Dannie wouldn't get into them. Or at least Mama would hear him first. She thought Papa might like to see her beautiful painted rose, so she placed it on his desktop. Her eye spotted Mama's pretty hand-painted plate, resting on a shelf above the desk. It had been there as long as she could remember. She studied it carefully. Its rim was covered with red and pink roses. She was sure she could paint a picture just like it. Maybe better. It couldn't be that hard to paint.

"Lily, we're waiting on you," Papa called from the other room.

Lily quickly ran to join the rest of the family and listen to Papa read the evening prayer from the little black prayer book. She half listened to Papa's deep voice, and half thought about what life would be like after she became a famous artist. Ice cream after dinner, every single day. A closet full of purple dresses. New books. Store-bought bread and deli meat in every school lunch.

She couldn't wait!

Tummy Troubles

Late one afternoon in early November, Lily was helping Mama tear an old dress into strips to make rag rugs. She heard a familiar squeaky sound and knew the mailman's truck was at the mailbox. She tossed the dress onto the floor and ran out the door as fast as she could. She wanted to get to the mailbox before Joseph did.

Joseph was hammering away in the woodworking shop, working on a project. He had heard the squeaky truck, too, and bolted out the door. He could run faster than Lily and beat her to the mailbox by just a few steps. So frustrating! She was the eldest and should be the first for everything.

Joseph pulled the mail out of the mailbox and slowly—oh so slowly—looked through every letter before handing it all to Lily with a smug grin. The thrill of beating her to the mailbox was over. He went back to the woodworking shop, hands in his pockets, whistling a tuneless tune.

Lily looked through all of the mail: a few letters, a catalog, and a picture postcard. She loved postcards. It was tempting to read what was written, especially since someone had drawn little pink flowers and twisty green vines in the bottom corners of the postcard. But Mama had told her that reading other people's mail was as bad as eavesdropping. Personally, Lily felt eavesdropping had some benefits. How else would she learn some interesting news? Just the other day, she discovered that Grandma had bunions. She wasn't sure what they were, but they sounded like a new type of vegetable from her garden.

Sometimes, Lily wished she weren't so curious, but she was. She was born that way. As she walked back to the house, she was sorely tempted to read the postcard, but of course it wasn't right. And she knew Mama was watching from the kitchen window.

Lily waited patiently as Mama read the postcard. "What does it say?"

Mama looked up. "Your cousin Esther is getting married and we are invited to her wedding."

"Uncle Ira's daughter, Esther?"

"Yes, do you remember her?"

Lily tried to think. She could remember visiting Grandpa Lapp's in Kentucky when she was still a little girl. She remembered Uncle Ira and Aunt Tillie. Who could ever forget Aunt Tillie and the Pow-Wow doctor she'd hired to cure Dannie's shyness? It didn't work, either. Dannie was still as shy as a mouse.

Lily tried and tried, but she couldn't put a face on Cousin Esther. Uncle Ira and Aunt Tillie had a big family of grown children—at least, they seemed grown-up to Lily, who had been only six.

But any wedding sounded like fun! It meant they would all go to Kentucky. "Are we going to go?"

"Papa and I will talk about it later," Mama said. "Put the mail on Papa's desk."

Later that day, Papa went through the day's mail. As he read the postcard, Lily waited right by his side.

"What do you think, Rachel?" he asked.

"Esther is your niece," Mama said. "If you'd like us to go, it's fine with me."

Papa put the card on the stack of letters. "I'll give it some thought."

Lily was disappointed. What was there to think about? It was a wedding and it would be fun. Sometimes, grown-ups seemed to make everything so serious and complicated. When she was all grown-up, she would make decisions right away. Would something be fun, or not fun? It was so simple.

A few days later, Mama told her that they had made a decision. Papa, Mama, Dannie, and baby Paul would go to the wedding but Lily and Joseph would have to stay at home.

Lily was stunned. Tears filled her eyes. How cruel! To be left alone while her family was off at a wedding?

Papa explained that they would have someone come stay with Lily and Joseph while they were away. "I'm sorry, Lily. I know you're disappointed. But it's more important for you to go to school than go to a wedding."

Lily was shocked senseless. Life just wasn't fair.

Lily helped Mama pack the big black suitcase with everything needed for the trip to Kentucky. She kept hoping Papa and Mama would change their minds. She even packed a grocery bag filled with her clothes, just in case. Maybe, if Papa couldn't find anyone to stay with them, they would be able to go. She would be ready.

But the evening before the trip, Papa drove off in the buggy and came home with Carrie Kauffman. Lily's hopes were dashed. Carrie climbed out of the buggy with her battered brown suitcase and walked toward the house. Carrie had come to stay with them after baby Paul had been born. Carrie had been nice. Maybe the situation wasn't quite so bleak. It was still a bitter disappointment to be left behind, but it wasn't quite so bleak.

The next morning, Lily woke and listened for the sounds of Mama in the kitchen. The house was strangely quiet. Then she remembered and felt an empty, sick feeling start in her toes and travel to her head. Papa, Mama, and the little boys had left for Kentucky while she had been sleeping.

Lily dressed quickly and hurried to wake Joseph. If allowed, he would sleep until noon. They followed Carrie out to the barn to do the morning chores. When it came to milking the cow, Carrie hesitated. "I've never milked a cow before," she said.

"How do you get your milk?" Joseph said.

"We buy it. We don't even own a cow."

What? How sad for Carrie! A cow was like a family member. Pansy was as important to Lily's family as Jim, the buggy horse. She could hardly remember a time without a cow.

Then a worry swooped in and replaced her pity for Carrie. Lily had never milked a cow, either. She had seen Papa and Mama do it more times than she could count. How hard could it be?

First, Pansy's udder needed washing with a special cleaner.

Lily sat on the little milking stool, feeling rather important, and got Pansy ready to be milked. She knew there was a certain way to milk a cow, a way to squeeze to get the milk to start, but her hands were small. She also knew that if a cow was milked wrong, it made her bind up and not lower the milk. She changed the plan. She had Carrie sit on the stool to try to milk Pansy. Carrie bit her lip, then started to milk. A few drops of milk plunked noisily into the pail. That wasn't how Mama milked Pansy—a big stream of milk would flow into the bucket. Lily and Joseph tried to show Carrie how to grab a teat, but they couldn't get much milk to come either. They kept taking turns trying to milk Pansy. Lily's forehead started to sweat. She was getting hotter and hotter though the morning was cold.

Pansy grew impatient. She could tell Carrie didn't know what she was doing. After a long while, Carrie decided they had enough milk. She took it inside to strain and cool it. Lily was surprised to see that even with all their hard work they had managed to get only a quart of milk. Mama and Papa usually got a gallon and a half. Lily had never seen such a pitiful show of milking a cow.

Lily was starving. She washed up for breakfast and happened to glance at the clock. It was already past time to leave for school. "Hurry, Joseph! We'll be late!"

Lily grabbed several bananas from the pantry and tossed them into their lunch pails. They could eat one on the way to school since they hadn't eaten breakfast before they left.

They ran all the way to school and got there just as Teacher Rhoda rang the bell. Lily slid into her desk breathless and panting. She tried not to think about Mama and Papa having fun on their trip. She tried not to think about poor Pansy, uncomfortable with a nearly full udder. She tried not to think about how dirty her dress was from the morning's milking—she hadn't had time to change for school. She thought she might stink a little too. Mostly, Lily tried not to feel sorry for herself for missing the wedding, but it was so hard! She had wanted to go so badly.

After school, Carrie tried to milk Pansy again. Two cats appeared out of nowhere, the way cats do, and tried to catch milk squirts when Carrie missed the bucket. *Pretty smart cats*, Lily thought. Papa would have shooed them away, but Carrie didn't say anything, so Lily let them stay. The cats were funny to watch. The milk would splash in their faces and then they would jump back as if they had been scalded. They would stop, lick the milk off, and start over. All in all, it made the milking go fast, though Carrie didn't get much more milk from Pansy than she had in the morning. Finally, they gave up and walked back to the house to make supper.

Lily and Joseph were both feeling very hungry. All they had eaten today were bananas. Lily didn't want to even think about bananas. She was sick of them.

Carrie was peeling potatoes to cook for dinner. Lily had a better idea for those potatoes. Mama always let them each have a small slice of raw potato sprinkled with salt to eat while they prepared supper. Those potatoes were so delicious. Tonight there was no reason they couldn't eat all the raw potatoes they wanted to. After all, they might as well try to make the most of their time with Carrie, since they were stuck at home. Mama and Papa and Dannie and Paul were having fun. Why couldn't they?

"Let's not cook the potatoes," Lily said.

Joseph's eyes lit up. "Yes, let's have a great big bowl full of raw potatoes for supper."

Carrie got the same look on her face as she did when she saw Pansy's big udder. Uncertain and a little confused. "I've never heard of such a thing."

Lily and Joseph both assured Carrie they loved eating raw potatoes, so she agreed, still looking hesitant. Lily happily placed a big bowl filled with raw potato slices on the table while Carrie dished out a bowl filled with steaming sweet corn and a platter of meat.

After they prayed a silent blessing, Lily reached for the bowl of raw potatoes and piled a big stack of them on her plate. She passed the bowl to Joseph. He piled an even bigger pile on his plate, then passed the bowl to Carrie. Carrie took a tiny slice. Just one. Lily thought Carrie was a little too timid. How could anyone not love raw potatoes?

Lily sprinkled salt on a slice and ate it. Delicious! It was every bit as crisp, slightly sweet, and crunchy as she knew it would be. She sprinkled another slice, ate it, then another and another. It wasn't long before her stomach felt funny. Joseph seemed to be having the same problem. They both took another slice and slowly ate it. That was enough. Soon Lily couldn't face one more bite of raw potato.

Carrie got a bowl and filled it with cold water and together they placed the remaining potato slices into it. They could stay in the refrigerator until tomorrow. She said she would fry them for dinner. Lily wasn't sure if she ever wanted to eat another slice of potato—cooked or raw. Bananas, either. She was done with bananas and potatoes for a long, long time.

As Lily got ready for bed that night, she felt tears start to roll down her cheeks. Carrie was nice, but she didn't know how to take care of children. She didn't know how to cook or milk a cow. She missed Mama and Papa. She even missed Dannie and Paul. Everything seemed strange—hollow and empty—without the sounds of Mama in the kitchen and Papa coming in from the barn one last time before he went to bed. She would never fall asleep tonight. Never. She was heartsick and tummy sick. She rubbed her tummy. It felt bloated and weird, like it might explode. She wondered if this was how poor Pansy was feeling tonight.

Green Hair and a Broken Plate

The smell of golden, crispy fried potatoes hung heavy in the kitchen air. Lily wasn't sure if she could stomach another potato, but Carrie didn't want last night's dinner of salted raw potatoes to go to waste. Carrie began to scoop potatoes out of a skillet and pile them into a bowl. "Lily, go outside and find Joseph and tell him it's time to wash up for lunch."

Lily ran out to the sandbox, expecting to find her brother, but it was empty. If Joseph wasn't in the sandbox, he would probably be on the swing. She ran around to the other side of the house. As she rounded the corner of the house, she stopped abruptly.

The barn had several long green streaks running down the front of it. She looked up and saw that the streaks started at the little loft door. The door was swinging back and forth in the breeze.

That could mean only one thing. Joseph was up to something.

Lily ran to the barn and went inside. As her eyes adjusted to the dim light, she heard footsteps in the hayloft. "Joseph! Lunch is ready."

"Uh, I'm not hungry." Joseph's voice floated down the hayloft stairs.

Something was wrong. Joseph never missed a meal. "What in the world happened to the barn?" Lily asked. "Why is it turning green?"

"I . . . uh . . . had a little accident."

"I'm going to go get Carrie!" Lily ran to the house to tell Carrie that there was an emergency in the barn.

Carrie looked horrified. "Is an animal hurt?"

"Oh no!" Lily said reassuringly. "It's only Joseph."

Carrie ran through the door and hurried to the barn. She called up the hayloft ladder. "Joseph, Joseph! Are you all right? Do you need help?"

Joseph's foot appeared on the top rung of the ladder. Then the other foot on the next rung.

Joseph didn't say a word until he reached the bottom of the ladder. Lily was stunned. He was covered, head to toe, in green paint. He stood there, blinking fast, looking at Lily and Carrie.

After a long, silent moment, Carrie snapped into action. She found an old washbasin and grabbed a towel that Papa used to wipe down Jim. She started to rub paint off Joseph. His face, then one arm, then the other.

"What happened?" Lily asked, as soon as she could find her voice.

"I thought I would paint a sign for the door to Papa's woodworking shop," Joseph started, spitting out paint. "I found just the right piece of wood and I used the paint Papa

had left over from the Whispering Pines sign. When I was finished, I opened the hayloft door so it would dry, but when I turned around, I slipped on the hay and my foot knocked over the stool that held the paint can. The can tipped over and splattered all over me."

"And down the side of the barn too," Lily added. She thought it was important to point that out.

Joseph was close to tears and Lily's comment pushed him over the brink. "I wanted it to be a surprise. A welcome back surprise." One tear leaked down his cheek.

"Don't cry, Joseph!" Carrie said, rubbing his green hair. "It will only make the paint run more."

Joseph had to strip out of his green clothes and run to the house wearing only Jim's wipe-down towel. At the kitchen sink, Carrie tried and tried to shampoo the paint out of Joseph's hair, but it still had an eerie greenish tinge to it. It almost glowed. Joseph looked miserable. Pansy was mooing from the barnyard, wanting to be milked, sounding miserable.

Lily felt miserable, too. The crispy, golden fried potatoes were now cold and soggy and gray. Another horrible meal. "Two more days," she thought to herself. At least, she didn't think she said it out loud—until she heard Carrie echo, "Just two more days."

Lily looked at Carrie, seated at the end of the table, rubbing the temples of her forehead like she was coming down with a frightful headache.

One more day. Just one more day and Mama, Papa, Dannie, and baby Paul would be home. Lily couldn't wait! She wanted to kiss baby Paul's fat cheeks and play hide-and-seek with Dannie. She missed hearing Papa's deep voice say, "Bedtime for little lambs." She had a long list of foods she wanted Mama to cook—nothing that included potatoes or bananas.

But she couldn't deny one very pleasant thing: Carrie didn't ask Lily to do any chores—no dishwashing, no garden work, no laundry. It was like a mini vacation for Lily.

After school, Lily settled into Papa's comfortable chair to finish reading a book. Out in the barn, Carrie was trying to milk poor Pansy and Joseph was supervising. The house was quiet. It was very peaceful. Lily turned the last page and closed the book, sad to come to the end. As she put the book away, her eyes caught Mama's pretty plate above Papa's desk. She'd forgotten about those paints in the pantry! Now would be a perfect time to paint—no little brothers around to bother her.

An idea started to blossom. A fine idea. She was going to try to paint roses just like the ones on that plate. She climbed up on Papa's desk and reached for the plate. She would have to be very careful with this plate. Papa had given it to Mama before they married. Mama said it was the most special plate she owned. She hardly ever used it as an actual plate. Mostly, it stayed on the shelf. Just for pretty, Mama said.

Lily held the plate carefully with both hands and turned around to get off the desk. Normally, she would jump off the desk. But not with Mama's special plate. Instead, she stepped carefully on Papa's swivel desk chair. When she put her weight on it, the chair seat twisted. The chair went rolling across the floor and Lily lost her balance. The plate flew out of her hands as she tumbled onto the floor. A terrible shattering sound made Lily cringe.

Slowly, Lily sat up and opened her eyes. Mama's beautiful plate had smashed into hundreds of little pieces.

As Lily started to pick up shards of ceramic, she heard Carrie and Joseph come into the house. Joseph stopped abruptly when he saw what she had done. "Oh Lily, you are going to be in so much trouble."

She scowled at him and his glowing green hair. But he was right. How could she tell Mama about the plate? Maybe

Mama wouldn't notice. If only she hadn't touched it in the first place.

Carrie set the half-filled pail of milk on the floor and went to get a broom and dustpan from the pantry. As she bent over to sweep the plate into the dustpan, Lily thought she heard her mutter, "One more day. Just one more day."

Out in the barnyard, Pansy let out a sorrowful moo.

Throughout the day, Lily glanced at the clock on the wall at the back of the schoolhouse. She did it so often that Aaron Yoder stuck his tongue out at her each time she swiveled her head around. She ignored him, as usual, because he was invisible to her. But the clock wasn't! Every hour that passed meant that Mama and Papa would be that much closer to home. When three o'clock came and Teacher Rhoda rang the dismissal bell, Lily and Joseph dashed out the door and raced down the road.

As they tore around the corner and up the driveway, Lily's heart leaped. Papa and Mama were home! She saw Papa crossing the yard with a big pail of milk in his hands. Dannie was trailing behind him, swinging a little pail. Mama was standing on the porch, baby Paul on her hip. It looked like any other day at Whispering Pines, but it wasn't! It was a very special day.

Papa scooped up Lily and Joseph for a big hug. Mama came down the porch steps to meet them. Baby Paul reached out for Lily when he saw her, which made her especially pleased. He hadn't forgotten her! And somehow, he looked bigger. Mama handed Paul to Lily and reached out to hug Joseph, accidentally knocking his black hat off. She looked shocked. "What happened to your hair?"

Dannie pointed to the barn. Long streaks of dried green paint ran down the front of it. "Your hair is the same color as the barn!"

"Where's Carrie?" Joseph asked, trying to steer the conversation away from green paint.

"She said she needed to get home and left very quickly," Papa said. "What exactly went on while we were away?" He was peering curiously at Joseph's green hair.

Joseph and Lily exchanged a look.

"I made a sign for you, Papa," Joseph said, pointing to the woodshop door. His sign was leaning on the top of the door, a little crooked.

PAPAS WUDWERK SHOPP

Lily cringed. Green paint dripped off the letters. Each word was spelled wrong. Joseph was a terrible speller. The worst speller in third grade.

Papa smiled. "It's a fine sign. Any chance the paint spilled while you were painting it?"

"Maybe," Joseph said quietly. Lily nodded.

"Anything else happen while we were away?" Papa said.

"Carrie had trouble milking Pansy," Lily volunteered.

"Yes, she told me about that," Papa said. He held up Pansy's pail—only half full. That was a worry. Cow's milk dried up quickly.

"And then Lily broke—" Joseph started, but Lily nudged him with her elbow, hard. This was her news to tell.

Mama was smiling, then her smile faded. "What did Lily break?"

Lily swallowed the lump in her throat. "I broke your pretty plate," she whispered.

Whispers grab hold of your attention like nothing else. Now Dannie was interested. He sidled between Mama and Papa so he could be closer to Lily.

"Which plate?" Mama asked. She got a strange, tight look on her face—the same kind of look Carrie had yesterday.

"The one on the shelf above Papa's desk," Lily said. "I wanted to try to paint roses just like the ones on the plate. I dropped it when I tried to get down."

Papa and Mama exchanged a look. "I think we'll have to put those paints away until you can be trusted to use them wisely," Mama said.

Later, Lily watched sadly as Mama packed up the paints and brushes that were tucked on a pantry shelf. For now, the box was going into the barn.

Lily thought Mama was being unfair. Joseph's green paint down the side of the barn and in his hair didn't seem to bother her as much as the broken plate. Lily hadn't meant to break the plate. But that was the trouble, right there. Lily never stopped to think of all that might happen until it happened.

Papa told Mama that he would find someone to paint another plate just like the one that was broken. Lily hoped he might also say that she could still use the paints and brushes, that it was a case of special circumstances since they had gone off to a wedding for a few days and were having fun— whereas Lily and Joseph were home with a babysitter who didn't know how to cook well and didn't know how to milk a cow—but he supported Mama's decision.

The happy homecoming had screeched to an abrupt halt. Still, Lily was glad her parents and little brothers were home and everyone was together again. And that night, there were no sorrowful moos out of Pansy.

One Chocolate Cupcake

The weather was changing. Frost feathers decorated the windowpanes in the morning, and children started wearing shoes to school, something done with great reluctance. During first recess, Lily watched Beth peel back the wrapper from a chocolate cupcake topped with fluffy white frosting and take a big bite. Lily could practically taste that sweet cupcake.

It had been a long time since Mama had baked cupcakes. Lily thought she'd make a tiny suggestion to Mama as soon as she got home from school. Mama might even tell her to go ahead and make some. Chocolate, of course. Chocolate cupcakes were the very best cupcakes of all. Lily's mouth watered just thinking about it.

As soon as Lily walked in the house after school, she hurried to find Mama. She looked in the kitchen, then the living room, but there was no sign of her. "Mama?" she called. She heard voices in the basement. She ran down the basement stairs and into Papa's woodworking shop. Mama was helping Papa steam wood to make curved chair backs. They looked up when they saw Lily.

"Can I bake some cupcakes?" Lily said.

Mama picked up the corner of her apron and wiped her forehead. "I just baked a big batch of chocolate chip cookies today. We should eat those before we bake something else. I don't want them to get stale."

Lily had no worries about chocolate chip cookies having a chance to get stale. Mama's cookies were legendary. She watched Papa and Mama work for a little while, wondering how to get Mama to change her mind.

"Could I make just one cupcake?" she asked.

Mama looked at her in surprise. "That might be hard to do."

"Let her try, Rachel," Papa said. "It would help her with long division."

Mama grinned. Lily complained bitterly about long division. "Okay. Go ahead. One batch of cake batter makes twenty cupcakes. You'll need to divide everything by twenty."

Lily ran upstairs and pulled Mama's blue *Amish Cooking* cookbook from the cupboard. She paged through it until she found the chocolate cupcake recipe.

She found a paper and pencil and sat down to figure out the measurements she would need to make one cupcake. First, she had to divide twenty into two cups of sugar. Oh no. This was harder than she had thought it would be.

And then there was water. She poured a cup of water into a bowl. She scooped the water out, tablespoon by tablespoon, into another bowl. She found out there were sixteen tablespoons in one cup. That would mean thirty-two tablespoons for two cups. If she divided that by twenty, it meant that she would need one full tablespoon and three-fifths of another one. Lily checked Mama's measuring spoons, but couldn't find one that was three-fifths, so she decided the half table-spoon would have to do.

She felt dizzy from all those numbers. All this dividing was harder than long division at school. Maybe she should rethink this. Immediately, the vision of a warm chocolate cupcake bounced in her head. She would keep going.

She measured the sugar and butter into her little bowl and mixed it. It was hardly enough to coat the wooden spoon. Lily looked at the recipe again. One egg. This was a puzzler. How could she divide an egg by twenty? And Mama wouldn't want her to waste one anyway so she decided this cupcake would have to skip its egg.

When the ingredients were mixed, Lily carefully scraped the little bit of batter into a cupcake liner. It looked lonely in a big muffin pan. She opened the oven door and slid the muffin pan inside and closed the door gently. She set the timer to make sure her little cupcake wouldn't burn. She had divided everything else by twenty so that must mean she would have to divide the baking time by twenty.

She smiled. That meant she would have to wait for only one minute before her cupcake was ready! When the minute was up, she pulled the cupcake out of the oven. It looked just like it did when she put it in the oven. She slid it back inside and ran to ask Mama how long she would have to bake it.

"It will still have to bake for twenty minutes," Mama said. "The cooking time wouldn't change."

Lily's cheeks flushed. Of course! She should have known that. Everybody knew that.

She hurried back upstairs to wait until her cupcake had finished baking. When the twenty minutes were over, she found several pot holders and carefully removed the cupcake to set it on the counter to cool. It didn't look as big and fluffy as she had hoped, but surely it would still taste good.

In the refrigerator, Lily found a bowl of leftover frosting. As soon as the cupcake had cooled, she spread the frosting on top of her cupcake. Finally, she took a bite.

Yuck!

It was awful! It didn't taste like any cupcake she had ever had. It was bitter and very rubbery.

She took it down to the shop to show it to Papa and Mama. "It doesn't taste good."

"Let me try it," Papa said. He took a bite and coughed.

"It's terrible, isn't it?" Lily said sadly.

"It tastes like an old shoe." Papa handed the cupcake to Mama but she shook her head.

"Did you ever taste a shoe?" Lily said. She tried to imagine him chewing on a shoe, but the thought was so funny that she started to giggle.

"No, I never did," he said. "But with all my brothers, I have smelled a few."

"At least you had fun trying to make a cupcake," Mama said. "Next week we can make a big batch."

That sounded like a good plan to Lily. "Chocolate?"

"Yes," Mama said. "And now you need to go clean up the kitchen."

Lily cringed. The sink was filled with dirty dishes. Making one cupcake used just as many dishes as if she had made twenty.

CHAPTER

19

Frozen Dannie

*L*ily looked longingly out the kitchen window. Snow swirled in thin, dancing ribbons through the trees. A light layer dusted the ground. The first snowfall of the year, and it was only the first week of December. She was aching to run out and play in the snow. Joseph and Dannie were already making little paths in it. Then they would pretend the paths were roads and run along them.

If only Saturday cleaning didn't have to be done every week. Then Lily could be out playing with them instead of dusting the furniture.

Upstairs, Mama was rocking baby Paul to sleep. Lily knew that as soon as Mama came back downstairs, she would have more chores in mind. She quickly whisked the dusting cloth over the front of Papa's big rolltop desk, dropped the cloth on his chair, and tiptoed quietly down the basement stairs.

She slipped into her coat and boots and ran outside. Joseph and Dannie were delighted to see her. After making a few more paths in the snow they decided to play horse. Dannie was youngest, so he would be the first to be a horse. Lily found her jumping rope on the porch and put it across Dannie's shoulders and under his arms. Joseph held the end of the rope and clucked "giddyup," and they trotted down one of the paths. Lily waited patiently for her turn, watching under the pine tree until they came back. The pine tree was the pretend barn. Its branches almost touched the ground on three sides. On the other side was the big air tank. The hook on the end made a nice place to tie their pretend horse.

When the boys came back, Joseph looped the rope through the hook. Dannie neighed and tried to paw his feet like a real horse. "The snow on the tank will be our pretend hay," Lily said.

Dannie licked a little. "It's good!" He licked some more.

Lily was getting ready to harness up Joseph when she heard a weird noise. Dannie had licked a patch of snow all the way down to the air tank. His tongue was stuck to it!

"Hold still while I get Mama," Lily said. She ran as fast as she could to the house, quickly kicked off her boots, and ran up the basement stairs. "Mama, Mama! Dannie needs you."

Mama had been mopping the floor and quickly put the mop back into the pail of water. "What's wrong with Dannie?"

"His tongue is stuck to the air tank," Lily said.

Mama quickly filled a pitcher with water. "Stay in the house in case Paul wakes up."

From the living room window, Lily watched Mama run to the air tank to rescue Dannie. Before she could reach him, Dannie fell to the ground with a howl. He cried so loud she was sure baby Paul would wake up and start to wail.

Mama scooped Dannie up in her arms and carried him

back to the house. As soon as they got inside, Lily asked if she could see Dannie's tongue.

Dannie stuck it out, in between sobs, and Lily gasped. She squeezed her eyes shut. Dannie's tongue was skinned and raw. Joseph examined the tongue. "He'll never be able to eat again," he said confidently, which made Dannie cry louder.

"Yes, Joseph, he will," Mama said.

"How could Dannie ever taste anything with his taste buds torn off?" Lily asked.

"His tongue will heal," Mama said. "It will hurt for a while, but after it's healed he should be able to taste and eat just fine."

At lunchtime, Papa put all of Dannie's food through Paul's baby food grinder. He would have to eat baby food until his tongue had healed enough to eat real food.

Lily felt a tiny bit responsible for Dannie's tongue accident. If she had stayed inside instead of sneaking out to play, Joseph and Dannie might not have thought of playing horse. If she hadn't said that the snow on the tank could be pretend hay, Dannie might not have thought to lick the snow off the air tank. But then she decided not to feel too badly. One thing she had learned about brothers—they were always thinking up things they shouldn't be doing.

The Gas Thieves

One morning Mama carefully set a gallon of fresh milk into the cold water to cool. "Daniel, we need more ice in the refrigerator," she said.

"I'll go start the ice compressor right away," Papa said. He took the gas can to the tank of gas under the pine trees to fill it up. Moments later, he returned to the house with a puzzled look on his face. "Was someone playing with the valve on the gas tank?"

Lily looked at Joseph who looked at Dannie who looked at Lily. Then they all looked at Papa and said, "No."

Papa stroked his beard. "I can't understand. The tank was filled up just a few weeks ago. This morning, there was barely enough gas to fill the gas can."

"Could it have a leak?" Mama asked.

"I checked," Papa said. "I couldn't find any sign of a leak." He shook his head. "It's a mystery to me. Now I'll have to order more gas. Hopefully, the gas truck can make a trip out tomorrow to fill the tank up or else we won't be able to keep ice in the refrigerator."

Thin gray clouds scuttled across the bleak sky. Lily held the ends of her shawl tightly in her hands, hoping to keep warm while walking home from school. She and Joseph were walking straight into a stiff, cold wind.

"Hurry, Lily," Joseph said as he ran ahead.

Lily tried to hurry, but it wasn't easy to run while one hand held her shawl together over her coat and the other hand held her lunch box. Joseph was far ahead of her, so she decided to let her shawl flap all it wanted to. She let it go and ran the rest of the way home. She couldn't wait to get inside the house and sit in the cozy kitchen. She hoped Mama would have a mug of steaming hot chocolate waiting for her.

Papa was in the kitchen when she reached the house. He took her lunch box from her so she could get warm by the stove. "I wouldn't be surprised if we wake up tomorrow morning and find quite a bit of snow on the ground. The air has that certain crisp smell—like a snowstorm is coming."

As Lily sipped hot chocolate and felt the warmth of the cup seep into her cold hands, she thought about snow. There had been spurts of snow in the last few weeks, but nothing sled-worthy. She hoped the snowstorm would be a big one and make the world look like a winter wonderland instead of a drab, gray, cheerless place. Snow games were so much more fun to play at recess.

Lily woke when she heard a loud bang: the basement door shutting. Papa must be heading out to the barn to do the morning chores.

She hopped out of bed, hurried to the window, held the curtain back with one hand, and peered outside. Everything looked white. Papa's forecast had been right! It had snowed. And snowed! Whispering Pines was covered with a white blanket.

Lily dressed and went downstairs to help Mama make breakfast. "Can we make ice cream when we come home from school?"

"Not tonight," Mama said. "Winter has only begun. There will be plenty of time to make ice cream."

Lily wished Mama liked ice cream making as much as she did. When she was a grown-up, she was going to make ice cream every single day that it snowed.

Papa came in from milking Pansy. He handed a pail of steaming frothy milk to Mama. "I think I know why the gas keeps disappearing from our gas tank," he said, a troubled look on his face. "There were tracks leading up to the tank. It looks like we have visitors during the night, and they're helping themselves to our gas."

Mama's eyes went wide. "How awful!"

Lily shivered. It was creepy to think some bad people were on their property in the night while they were all sound asleep. "Are you going to call the police?"

Papa and Mama exchanged a glance. "No," Papa said quickly. "I'll see if I can catch them myself."

Lily wondered what Papa would do if he caught the thieves. A policeman would take the thieves to jail and lock them up. Thieves would stay in jail until they learned not to take things that didn't belong to them. She had read about it in a book, so she knew it was true. Maybe Papa would lock them up in the woodshed. That would be a good place to keep the gas thieves. Lily imagined carrying bread and water out to feed them so they wouldn't starve. She pictured them handing out pieces of Papa's cut wood for the family to use in the house. She wondered how long it would take the bad men to repent of their ways. Maybe . . . until next summer?

That evening Papa didn't go to bed when it was bedtime. Instead, he blew out the lights and sat next to one of the kitchen windows so that he could watch and see who came to get gas. Lily and Joseph volunteered to stay up with him and help, but he sent them to bed. "No need for three people to be tired and cranky in the morning," he told them. But Papa was never tired and cranky. Joseph was, but Papa never was.

The next morning, Lily hurried downstairs to see if Papa caught the thieves. He shook his head. "No one came to get gas last night. I'll watch again for a while tonight. I'm sure they'll be back. It seems like they have a habit of helping themselves."

"Will you lock them up in the woodshed?" Lily asked.

Papa gave her a surprised look. "No, if I wanted to lock them up, I would call the police. There are other ways to deal with people instead of locking them up."

❧✖❧

Several nights later, Lily woke with a start. She heard Papa's hurried footsteps and a click as the basement door shut. It scared her to think of Papa capturing the gas thieves. What if they were very bad men? What if they had a big shotgun and pointed it at Papa like the neighbor in New York did?

She threw the covers back and went to the window to see what was going on outside. She could see two figures—older than boys but younger than men—bent over the valve of the gas tank, filling up a gas can. In the moonlight, she saw Papa walk toward them, a gas can in one hand. For a long while, the big boys didn't know he was there. They startled when they realized they were being watched. Papa talked to them for a long while. Then, the boys walked off down the road. She saw Papa head back to the house with his gas can.

Lily felt disappointed. Nothing had happened! Papa had not caught the thieves. He'd only talked to them. Anyone could do that.

The next morning, while everyone was eating breakfast, Papa told the story of what had happened. "I caught the thieves in the act last night."

With a mouthful of food, Joseph said, "Who were they?"

"They were Mr. Beal's teenagers," Papa said. "I offered them a can of gas. I told them if they ever needed gas, they could come up to the house and ask for it and I would be happy to give it to them. That way they don't have to steal it."

Lily tore her buttered toast into tiny pieces. She still felt disappointed. What if those bad boys kept coming back? It bothered her that anyone would steal from Papa. She knew how hard her parents worked. Those bad boys didn't work hard at all. "Aren't you even going to tell Mr. Beal what his bad boys did?"

Papa took his time answering. "They aren't bad boys, Lily. They did a bad thing. There's a difference." He sprinkled salt and pepper over his scrambled eggs. "They seemed embarrassed to have been caught. I have a feeling our gas won't be disappearing any longer."

Lily hoped he was right. A little part of her wished those bad boys had been locked up in the woodshed until they learned their lesson.

Christmas at Whispering Pines

"Christmas is coming tomorrow! Christmas is coming tomorrow!" Dannie sang the same phrase over and over as he ran through the house. Lily felt like skipping along behind him and joining him in his happy little song.

Christmas was finally almost here. She had been looking forward to it for so long. She thought of the gift for Papa and Mama she had hidden in one of her desk drawers. She had worked long and hard on that gift and was pleased with how it turned out.

It had started with a simple piece of cardboard that she had covered with scraps of wallpaper. She wrote a special poem about Papa and Mama on it. All around the border were pretty stickers.

Teacher Rhoda gave a sticker to anyone who received 100 percent on their arithmetic tests. Lily didn't like arithmetic but she needed those stickers to make a border for the poem.

For weeks, she had worked hard to make sure she didn't get a single math problem wrong and her efforts had paid off. The poem was framed in stickers. She felt sure that Papa and Mama would love it. It was a gift of extreme hardship and sacrifice.

Dannie made another lap through the house. "Christmas is coming tomorrow! Christmas is coming tomorrow!"

Lily carried a bowl filled with layered pudding into the pantry, set it on the shelf, and stood back to admire it. It looked so pretty. There was a layer of green Jell-O at the bottom and red on the top with white fluffy cream cheese in the middle.

The entire pantry looked like a store. Its shelves were filled with food. There were pies, cookies, several different kinds of bread, and glass gallon jars filled with Christmas treats of party mix, caramel corn, and different homemade candies and snacks. Mama had been working hard to get everything ready for Christmas.

Lily knew if she opened the refrigerator she would see even more food for tomorrow's feast. They would take everything over to Grandma and Grandpa Miller's house for Christmas dinner. Uncle Elmer's family and Uncle Jacob's family were going to be there too. Lily could hardly wait.

"Christmas is coming tomorrow! Christmas is coming tomorrow!" Dannie was still singing.

"I think everything is ready for Christmas," Mama said, growing weary of Dannie's tuneless song. "Lily, take your brothers outside and ride sleds until suppertime."

Somehow, upstairs, singing at the top of his lungs, Dannie heard Mama mention sledding. He galloped downstairs and grabbed his coat. Lily slipped into her own coat, helped Dannie tug on his boots, and went to find Joseph in the shop. Lately, that's where Joseph could be found, watching Papa work.

They dragged their sleds to the top of the small hill behind the barn. Joseph sat on his sled and Dannie jumped on it behind him. They went zooming down the hill laughing and squealing all the way.

Lily sat on her sled and wiggled a little to make it start moving. Soon she was flying down the hill. Joseph and Dannie waited at the bottom for her, and then they all walked up together. This time Dannie rode down the hill with Lily.

After several more rides, Dannie wanted to ride a sled all by himself. "Joseph can ride with Lily."

"You're too little, Dannie," Lily said.

"I'm *not* too little." He grabbed the rope from Joseph's sled and pulled it farther up the hill. "I can pull it by myself and I can ride by myself, too!"

Lily didn't want to argue with Dannie. He could be stubborn. Plus, tomorrow was Christmas. She didn't want anything to spoil her happy mood, especially not a mad little brother. Reluctantly, she agreed to give Dannie a turn.

Dannie hopped on the sled, headfirst, and started down the hill. The sled swerved back and forth. Then it straightened out . . . and headed straight toward the barn! Lily froze. She watched in horror as Dannie crashed into the side of the barn. For a long, long moment, there was silence. Then . . . Dannie started to howl like a wounded coyote.

Lily and Joseph ran as fast as they could to get to him. Lily nearly gagged when she saw his face—bloody and scraped up, and his nose looked crooked. Joseph screamed, which only got Dannie howling louder. Lily ran to the workshop as fast as she could to tell Papa that Dannie had had an accident and might be dying.

Papa flew to the barn. He came back to the house with

Dannie in his arms, still wailing. Mama helped him out of his coat. Papa carried him to the kitchen to wash the blood off his face and see how badly he was hurt. Apparently, he wasn't dying.

Mama and Papa talked softly to Dannie as they cleaned him up. "There now, we'll let you sit on my chair while Mama reads a book to you," Papa said in his gentlest voice. Dannie's breath was still coming in sobs, but slower.

Another wave of sickness hit Lily when she looked at Dannie. He had a bump on his head and his lips were swollen. Worst of all, his two front teeth were missing.

Mama scribbled a note and handed it to Lily. "Go take this to Grandma Miller," she said. She started to read Dannie's favorite book to him while Lily wrapped up in her coat and bonnet. She trudged up the road to Grandma's house. She thought about peeking at the note, like she often did, but she didn't even want to know what that note said.

When Grandma read the note, she seemed disappointed. She patted Lily's cold cheek. "Tell Dannie that I'm sorry he is hurt. We'll miss you tomorrow. I'll make sure to save some leftovers for you."

Lily walked home, tears streaming down her cheeks. It was just what she feared! She wouldn't be going to the special family dinner tomorrow. She wouldn't get to play with Hannah and Aunt Susie. She would eat crummy old leftovers. She wished they would never even have gone sledding—and certainly not let Dannie try to ride by himself. Now Christmas was ruined.

By the time she got home, Mama was bustling around the kitchen again. Papa had moved his big chair into the kitchen for Dannie. He was sitting on it surrounded with blankets and his favorite books.

Lily suggested to Mama, in the tiniest way, that she and Papa and Joseph could still go to Christmas dinner tomorrow.

Mama silenced her with a look. "Certainly not. Christmas is about being with our family. If one of us can't go, we will all stay at home." She arched one eyebrow in that way she had. Lily thought she sounded a little crisp.

That was the end of the discussion.

The next morning, the sun shone brightly. "Looks like we'll all have a very nice day at home," Papa said when he came in from doing the chores. "I think it's going to be the best Christmas we have ever had." He washed his hands and scooped swollen, bruised Dannie up in his arms and sat on his chair with him. He whistled "O Beautiful Star of Bethlehem" while Mama finished getting breakfast ready.

Lily loved Christmas breakfast. Mama made special dishes and each child was given an orange. As soon as they were done eating, Lily helped Mama clear the plates away as Papa read the story of the first true Christmas from the Bible. Mama and Lily worked quietly so they wouldn't miss a word. Lily loved hearing Papa's deep rich voice as he read. He had a fine reading voice, Papa did.

When Mama had the kitchen sparkling clean again, Papa carried Dannie upstairs. Lily held Paul and followed Joseph, who was right behind Papa. The children waited in Lily's room. So exciting! The time had come for Papa and Mama to get their gifts ready for the children.

"Let's play Sorry! until it's time to go downstairs," Joseph said. Lily got the game ready and they started to play, even though Dannie and baby Paul didn't really know how to play. They were just getting involved as Papa knocked on Lily's bedroom door. He had a big grin on his face. "Present time!" He carried Dannie downstairs. Lily thought Dannie was lucky to be carried everywhere. At least there was one good thing about sledding straight into a barn.

In the kitchen, Lily quickly sat at her place and peered at the towel in front of her seat. Under it were her gifts. She wanted to peek under her towel but knew she shouldn't. She had to be an example to her little brothers and wait until everyone else was ready. But oh, how she wanted to peek! Papa sat at the head of the table. He was smiling from ear to ear. "Okay, let's see what you children might have."

Lily lifted her towel. There was a new china bowl filled with candy and nuts. It would replace the glued-together one that Paul had broken. There was a new book. And a pack of beautiful stationery, almost too pretty to use. She would use it only to write to Grandma Lapp.

Lily had forgotten her gift for Mama and Papa! She ran upstairs, grabbed it from her desk, hurried back down, and thrust it into Papa's hands. He held the framed poem up against the light to read it and then showed it to Mama. Lily described the painful arithmetic quizzes she had endured just to get those stickers. Mama took the poem into her bedroom and placed it on top of her dresser. So she could see it every day, she said, and think of Lily working so hard at school.

So far, Christmas had been much better than she had expected after the Dannie Disaster. Lily tucked her new pack of stationery into one of her desk drawers, far in the back, where her brothers wouldn't find it. She got her new book and went downstairs to settle into a corner of the sofa. She tried not to think about the Christmas dinner that her entire—*entire*!—extended family was enjoying. Whenever images of their happy feast popped into her mind, she tried to push the thought away. Over and over. She was stuck on page one of her book, rereading and rereading while pushing images of the Miller feast away, when a knock came on the door.

Papa was first to open the door, with Lily right on his heels. There on the porch were Grandpa, Grandma, and Aunt Susie! Behind them were Uncle Elmer's and Uncle Jacob's families. Everyone! Everyone was here!

Grandma had a big grin on her face. "We decided since you couldn't come to us for Christmas dinner, we would bring Christmas dinner to you."

Papa and Lily were stunned.

"Well, aren't you going to let us in?" Grandpa said, stamping his feet from the cold.

Papa opened the door as wide as he could. The Miller family flowed in, carrying bowls and dishes and platters into the kitchen. The women got right to work. They helped Mama put extension boards into the table and set it with her prettiest dishes. Everyone was laughing and talking as they prepared dinner and then sat down together to eat it.

During dinner, Lily looked around the table. There was more food than anyone could ever eat and everyone was talking and the gas lights made the room look sparkly. And they were all together. Happiness welled up in Lily and she knew she would never forget this moment. It was the best Christmas ever.

The Snow Cave

*E*verywhere Lily looked there was snow and more snow. As she bundled up for a buggy ride to school, Papa told her that last night's snowstorm had brought snow more than two feet deep.

As much as Lily liked how beautiful everything looked covered in snow, she knew it would create a problem at school. The children wouldn't be able to play Fox and Geese at recess. That was Lily's favorite winter game.

During the first recess, the girls stayed inside to play games or piece a puzzle together rather than try to play in the deep snow. The boys, naturally, were excited about all the snow. Levi, Aaron Yoder, and Sam Stoltzfus had each brought a shovel along to school. They took turns digging a cave in the big drift of snow beside the schoolhouse.

Lily and Hannah stood at the window, watching those silly boys dig, but they soon grew bored and joined the girls.

At lunch, the only thing the boys could talk about was the snow cave. "We should get it done today," Aaron said, "and then we can have fun sitting inside of it."

"I get to have the first turn," Levi said. "After all, I brought the biggest shovel to school. It's only fair that I get to go first."

Lily was surprised that the boys readily agreed to let Levi go first. She was glad they were getting along and not letting Levi's endless bragging become too aggravating. Though, even to Lily, it was.

At the window, the girls watched the boys finish digging out the cave. After the boys were satisfied that the cave was finished, they stuck their shovels in the snow. They huddled together for a moment to discuss something, then Levi ran to the stairs of the schoolhouse basement and disappeared. He reappeared with a flying saucer. Lily watched as he placed it carefully in front of the cave. A door!

The boys stood back to admire their work. Then Levi yanked the flying saucer away and crawled into the cave. The second his feet disappeared from sight, Sam Stoltzfus repositioned the flying saucer at the opening. Aaron and a few other boys started shoveling snow in front of it as fast as they could.

Lily *knew* they were up to something! The boys hadn't been nice to let Levi go in first—they did it so they could trap him inside of the cave.

Hannah and Lily ran to Teacher Rhoda to tell her what the boys were doing. Teacher Rhoda hurried to get her coat on, but before she could get her arm through a sleeve, a loud yell filled the air. They ran to the window and saw the boys stampeding over the cave so the roof would collapse on Levi.

Teacher Rhoda ran outside to rescue Levi. Lily watched at

the window, horrified. He was completely buried in the snow. Finally, a gloved hand emerged, then an arm, and Teacher Rhoda yanked hard and Levi's head popped up. He looked dazed, blinking like a newborn owl. Teacher Rhoda pulled him out of the snow pile and helped to brush him off. Once he was safely inside the schoolhouse, she rang the bell. Thanks to Aaron Yoder and Sam Stoltzfus, recess would be cut short today.

The students slipped quietly to their desks. Aaron and Sam had goofy grins on their faces but Teacher Rhoda did not look amused at all. The air in the schoolhouse felt dreadful to Lily, heavy and threatening, like right before a tornado touched down. Something terrible was about to happen.

Teacher Rhoda kept her eyes on her desk for a long, long moment. Then she lifted her chin. "Put your books away for school dismissal."

Lily looked at the clock. It was much earlier than usual and Mama would be surprised to see them. But Lily was glad to get away from this heavy atmosphere.

Teacher Rhoda stood. "Everyone may go home except for Aaron Yoder, Sam Stoltzfus, and anyone else who was involved in trapping Levi inside that snow cave."

Lily quickly got her shawl and bonnet, grabbed her lunch box off the shelf, and followed Hannah out the door. There was one good thing about this terrible ordeal: finally Hannah had seen for herself how awful Aaron Yoder truly was. Lily would no longer have to listen to Hannah go on and on about how wonderful and cute and smart Aaron was. Her dearest friend and cousin had a horrible and completely un-understandable crush on Aaron Yoder. She thought he was a hero. Lily knew he wasn't. He was a terrible, awful boy.

The two girls trudged slowly through the snow. "I don't think Teacher Rhoda should have made Aaron stay after school," Hannah said.

Lily stopped in her tracks. Wait. *What?* "Aaron trapped Levi inside that snow cave and then helped jump on top of it to make it collapse on top of him."

"He was only going along with what the other boys were doing."

Lily couldn't believe her ears. "Levi is your brother!"

"Still, I don't think Aaron meant to be mean."

"You must be crazy!" she exclaimed in her most understanding way. "Of course he meant to be mean! Everything he does is mean!"

Hannah dismissed Lily's complaints with a wave of her hand. "I still think he is the nicest boy in school."

That was the last straw. Lily slapped her on the cheek, hard. Hannah's eyes widened and her mouth opened to an O. A red handprint appeared on Hannah's face. Then she started to cry.

Lily was horrified. She had slapped Hannah! It was all Aaron Yoder's fault.

Hannah started toward home, tears running down her face. When they came to the fork in the road where Hannah turned off to head to her house, she split off without a word, still crying. Lily was grateful Joseph had run ahead with Levi and had not seen what had happened with Hannah. She walked slowly the rest of the way home, feeling ashamed. Why, she was almost as bad as mean-hearted Aaron Yoder. Not quite, but almost.

She wiped away a tear before she walked into Papa's woodworking shop. He looked up when he heard the door open, but his cheerful smile faded away when he saw Lily. "Sit down and tell me everything."

How did Papa know something was wrong? Lily sat on the stool and told him all that had happened at school. She described how the boys had tricked Levi to trap him. "All Hannah ever talks about is Aaron Yoder and how wonderful he is." She dropped her chin to her chest and mumbled, "So then I might have given Hannah a tiny little slap."

Papa lifted his dark eyebrows. "Slapping Hannah didn't really solve anything, did it?"

Tears pricked Lily's eyes. "No. It made both of us cry."

"Take your lunch box to the kitchen. Then we'll go over to Hannah's and you can apologize for losing your temper."

Lily wished she had not slapped Hannah, but she wasn't sorry enough to want to apologize. She took her lunch box upstairs, placed it on the kitchen counter, and took a long, slow drink of water. Then another. As slowly as she could.

Papa appeared at the top of the stairs, wondering what had happened to her. "Ready?"

They trudged through the deep snow to get to Hannah's house. Papa knocked on the door. Aunt Mary came to the door, surprised to see Papa standing beside Lily. She invited them to come in out of the cold.

"Lily has something she wants to say to Hannah," Papa said.

Aunt Mary asked them to take a seat in the living room. She called up the stairs to Hannah and then went back to work in the kitchen.

Hannah came downstairs and stopped abruptly when she saw Lily and Papa. Lily rose from her chair. "I'm sorry that I slapped you."

Hannah rubbed her cheek. "That's okay. It stopped sting-
ing after I got home."

They stood, awkwardly, looking at the floor. Hannah took
a step closer to Lily. In a low voice, she said, "I won't talk
about Aaron anymore. I like you better than him."

Lily was so happy to hear that! She threw her arms around
Hannah.

Papa cleared his throat, then coughed, then finally clapped
his hands. "I'm glad you girls got everything patched up. It's
never good to let the sun go down on anger. But now it's time
to go home. Mama needs Lily's help with supper. You girls
can play with each other tomorrow."

On the way home, Lily's feet felt light and happy, even
though the snow was just as deep to trudge through. She and
Hannah were friends again. But she did hope that Hannah's
taste in boys would improve as she got older.

23

Fire at the Schoolhouse!

It was a bitterly cold morning in late January. Wind howled around the corners of the house and whistled through the windows. Snow piled up in deep drifts in front of the door. "The wind has a mean bite to it," Papa said as he scraped the last bit of porridge out of baby Paul's little bowl and fed it to him. "I think it's too cold for Lily and Joseph to walk to school. What do you think, Rachel?"

Mama peered at the thermometer that hung outside the kitchen window. "It's only eight degrees," she said. "The wind will make it feel much colder. I'll get their lunches packed while you get Jim hitched up."

"Can I ride along?" Dannie said.

Lily sighed when she heard him ask that question. Dannie was getting to be such a tag-along. If he came, there wouldn't be enough room for everyone on the front seat with Papa. She would be the one to sit alone in the back because she was the oldest. She would be alone and cold. She hoped Papa would say that it was too chilly for Dannie to come, but he didn't. "If you bundle up warmly you can ride along," Papa told Dannie. He helped Dannie with his jacket and crouched down to close the hooks and eyes on his coat. "You'll be able to keep me company on the ride back home." Papa plucked his hat off the wall peg and headed out to the barn.

Lily hadn't considered that it might be a lonely drive home for Papa after dropping them at school. She felt a tiny pinch of guilt for not wanting Dannie to tag along.

Lily hopped into the back of the buggy and was pleased that Joseph climbed in beside her. They covered their laps with the thick, fuzzy buggy robes, but it wasn't long before Lily's toes were cold. Her breath made big puffy white clouds. She and Joseph tried to see who could make the biggest breath cloud.

In the front seat, Dannie chattered away to Papa. Lily didn't even try to listen to what he was saying. Dannie had a lot to say but most of it wasn't very interesting to Lily. Fortunately, Papa was one of the best listeners in the world. He always seemed to enjoy listening to whatever anyone had to say. Even Dannie.

Jim trotted slowly through the wind and the snow. The buggy wheels squealed as they cut through the snow. It was a sound unique to a winter day, and even though Lily liked the snow on the ground, she knew that it took more work for Jim to pull the buggy.

As they crested the last hill before the schoolhouse, Dannie eyes went wide. "Look at all the fire trucks!" he said. "Look! The schoolhouse is burning!"

Lily threw the buggy robe off her lap and stood to look

out the storm front. Dannie was right! The schoolhouse was burning. Flames licked at the roof around the chimney. More fire trucks than she had ever seen were parked in the school yard and beside the road. Red lights flashed everywhere. A few firefighters held a big hose and sprayed water on the fire. Lily couldn't look at it any longer and squeezed her eyes shut. Oh, how terrible! The schoolhouse was burning. They couldn't have school without a schoolhouse.

Then came a horrible, terrible realization. Her box of

beautiful crayons was in that schoolhouse! They would be destroyed. Melted into wax.

Lily would never forget the day when Mama gave the crayons to her. She had just come back from town after buying Lily and Joseph's school supplies. Mama reached into her shopping bag and gave Joseph a brand-new pack of twenty-four crayons. Lily loved new crayons. She waited for Mama to give her a new pack, just like Joseph's. Instead, Mama pulled out a pack of sixty-four crayons and handed them to Lily. Sixty-four! She was stunned, speechless. Too happy for words.

Lily spent hours looking through her box of brand-new crayons, memorizing each name: aquamarine, topaz, sunset orange. Even the names were beautiful.

"You're growing up, Lily," Mama said. "You're old enough to have a box of sixty-four crayons. Since fourth graders don't color very often, I expect you to keep these crayons nice. They should last for the rest of your school years."

Lily had tried to keep these sixty-four crayons from breaking or smudging against each other. She kept the points nice and sharp. She would miss getting a brand-new box of crayons every year but having one box of sixty-four was better than a new box of twenty-four.

Joseph and Dannie looked at Lily's box of crayons with longing in their eyes. And they didn't even like to color! For the first time in Lily's life, she had something she was not expected to share. When Joseph and Dannie reached fourth grade, Mama said they would get their very own box of sixty-four crayons as well.

Lily had felt important on the first Friday afternoon art period when she took her box of beautiful crayons out of her desk and used them. None of her friends had a big box of crayons. Beth, Malinda, and Hannah admired them, and Effie said that they were too worldly, but Lily was sure that Effie wished she had such a box of crayons.

It always took Lily a long time to color pictures. There were so many different colors to choose from and she wanted to take better care of these crayons than she ever had with her other crayons. They needed to last five years, until she would be finished with school and all grown-up.

But now, as she thought about her beautiful crayons melting in the schoolhouse fire, she wished she had colored with them every day.

Papa pulled Jim to the side of the road. A policeman came up to the buggy. "There won't be any school today," he told Papa. The two men talked a little more and then Papa turned Jim and the buggy around to head for home.

"Couldn't we get my box of crayons out of the schoolhouse?" Lily asked.

Papa turned to look at her. "Your what?"

"My box of sixty-four crayons," Lily said. "I don't want them to be burned."

Papa gave her a sharp glance. "I would never ask anyone to go inside a burning building just to get a box of crayons."

Of course. Of course he wouldn't do that. Lily felt embarrassed that she had even asked such a thing. What was she thinking?

As soon as they reached home, Dannie ran inside to tell Mama the exciting news about the fire trucks and the burning schoolhouse. He always had to be first, Dannie did.

Mama looked concerned. "I'm grateful the fire didn't start when the children were in school."

Lily hadn't even stopped to think about something like

that. How terrible it would be to be trapped inside a school-house with a fire on the roof. She felt another pinch of guilt. She had been getting all kinds of pinches of guilt today, and it was only morning.

Later that day, Papa hitched Jim to the buggy and went to pick up Grandpa Miller and Uncle Jacob. They wanted to see if there was anything they could do at the schoolhouse. They were gone a long time. Lily kept running to the window to see if Papa was coming home. She wanted to hear if the firemen had been able to stop the fire.

Mama was sewing at her sewing machine. She gave Lily a headscarf to hem by hand. As Lily sewed, she felt very sorry for herself. This had been a terrible day. First, the fire at the schoolhouse. Second, she didn't know if her box of crayons had survived. Third, she had to sit home and hem a headscarf by hand. She hated to sew. This day was almost too much to bear.

When Lily heard the squeak of buggy wheels in the snow, she dropped the headscarf she had been working on and ran to the window. Papa was pulling up to the barn. "I'm going to help Papa unhitch," she said, and darted down to the basement to get her coat and boots before Mama could tell her to stay inside and finish the headscarf.

By the time Lily reached him, Papa had already unhitched Jim and was pushing the buggy into the barn. Lily followed Papa into the barn as he led Jim into a stall. She blinked her eyes to try to adjust to the barn's dim light. Papa curried and brushed Jim, a way to thank him for being such a good buggy horse. Lily stayed quiet as long as she could—at least a full minute. But she had to know! "Did the firemen save the schoolhouse?"

"It didn't burn to the ground, but the damage is bad. We need to tear down the entire building and build a new one. Everyone is planning to lay all their other work aside so by Monday, Lord willing, there will be a new schoolhouse for all of you children."

So it was true. Lily's box of sixty-four beautiful crayons had been ruined. She knew it wasn't right to care more about the crayons than she did for the schoolhouse. The thing was—the crayons had been her very own, and the schoolhouse had been shared with everyone.

She walked slowly back to the house, kicking and scuffing the fluffy snow. It was only Tuesday. Monday was a long way off. She hoped that Mama wouldn't ask her to do more hand sewing. There was nothing that she hated as much as hand sewing. Even putting up with Aaron Yoder and Effie Kauffman at school was better than hand sewing.

CHAPTER

24

Starting Over

*E*arly Wednesday morning, Lily helped Mama pack lunch for Papa. He was going to help the rest of the men in the community build a new schoolhouse. It would take a few days to complete, so each day would be a work frolic. Usually, large meals were part of the frolics, but not this time. Each person was asked to pack his own lunch to take along.

Lily spooned some peaches into a dish and carefully covered it. She set it into a corner of Papa's lunch box while Mama fit in several sandwiches. There was still space to tuck a few cookies. Then Lily closed the lid. She hoped Papa would have enough to eat so that he wouldn't get too hungry before suppertime. She worried that the men wouldn't be able to work very fast if they got too hungry. She wanted them to work quickly so she could go back to school.

By the time Uncle Elmer drove into the driveway with his horse and buggy, Papa had his tools and lunch box, ready to go. Lily stood at the window and watched as Papa tucked his tool belt under the seat and then climbed on the buggy. They drove down the road to pick up Grandpa and Uncle Jacob.

Lily wandered around the house aimlessly trying to decide what to do for the rest of the day. Her favorite books and her doll didn't seem very exciting. Since the fire, all she wanted to do was to color with her beautiful box of crayons. How sad. Why was it that the one thing you wanted most, you could never seem to have?

Joseph didn't mind that he couldn't go to school. He and Dannie played in the snow for a while and built a snowman. After that, they set up their toy farms in the corner of the living room and became thoroughly involved in the game of pretend farming.

Lily made another round through the kitchen and living room.

Mama could tell Lily felt antsy. "You could work on your cross-stitching."

Oh *no*. Lily knew that she should enjoy cross-stitching as much as other little girls her age, but she hated it. It was so tedious to use a needle and thread by hand. Over and over, the same little *x* for a cross-stitch. "Maybe I could sew on the sewing machine," she said, hoping Mama would forget about the cross-stitching. She liked the sewing machine because it was noisy and fast, but Mama didn't have anything for her to sew on the sewing machine.

Mama got the square of fabric that Lily had been working on to make a pretty pillow top. In each corner, there were several hearts made with little *x*'s and three flowers. Lily sat down and threaded her needle with purple embroidery floss and took several stitches. "Cross-stitching is not fun!" she said, mostly to herself, and jabbed the needle into the fabric again. She jabbed too hard and pricked her finger. A little drop of blood stained the fabric. "Ouch!" Lily quickly put her finger in her mouth.

Mama crossed the room to see what had happened. She saw a drop of red on the fabric. "Let's go take care of this right away before the blood sets in the fabric." Mama hurried to get a bottle of peroxide from the medicine cabinet. She started dabbing the fabric with a cloth soaked in peroxide. Lily sat on the sofa, feeling more gloomy than she did when she started to cross-stitch. Mama was more worried about the fabric than she was about the gigantic hole Lily had poked into her finger.

After Mama was satisfied that the blood drop on the fabric had been washed away, she came back into the living room. For a moment, she gazed thoughtfully at Lily. "I don't think your mind is on the things you can do here at home. Why don't you bundle up and go spend the rest of the day with Grandma and Aunt Susie."

Instantly, Lily felt a happy mood return. Mama did understand! She ran to get her coat, shawl, and bonnet and started up the road. It was snowing and the wind blew right in her face, but as long as she kept her head down and walked fast, she didn't mind the cold too much.

Grandma and Aunt Susie were pleased to answer the knock on the door and find Lily. "Come in, come in out of the cold," Grandma said.

Lily stepped inside and removed her boots. She was careful not to let any snow stay on the floor. It would never do to make melted snow puddles on Grandma's floor.

Aunt Susie took Lily's wraps and hung them on a hook. "Do you want to help me color?" she asked, a hopeful look on her sweet, childlike face.

Oh, how wonderful! She would get to color today, after all. Lily followed Aunt Susie to help her choose which coloring books to color in. Aunt Susie had a big stack of coloring books. Lily took her time looking at each one before settling on one with baby animals.

They took the books and crayons to the kitchen table and sat down to begin coloring. Grandma was baking an apple pie. She looked at Lily and said, "Your nose is still red from the cold walk you had to our house. It looks as if you need some hot chocolate." She set two mugs of steaming hot chocolate on the table for Lily and Aunt Susie. Then, just for fun, she sprinkled a few mini-marshmallows on top.

Lily felt warm and cozy and special as she stirred her hot chocolate and took a few tiny sips. This day had started so bleak and was improving by the minute. Papa was helping all the other men build a new schoolhouse, and she could spend all afternoon at her Grandma's house, coloring with her favorite aunt. And no little brothers! It was pure bliss.

Grandma sent Lily home in plenty of time to help Mama prepare supper. Papa walked up the driveway just as the sun was setting and dinner was ready to be served. Lily had just set a bowl of fried potatoes on the table as Papa washed up at the sink. He had a pleased look on his face. "Is the new schoolhouse finished?" Lily asked.

"Not quite," he said. "Tomorrow we should finish up. On Friday, we'll be moving in desks while the school board goes and buys new books. You and Joseph can go back to school on Monday."

Lily felt excited. She loved going to school. Having a

brand-new schoolhouse would be fun. And new books would be nice, too. She wondered if Teacher Rhoda would make the children start all over again with the workbooks. That didn't sound like much fun. But then a happy thought danced through Lily's mind, something that hadn't occurred to her: she would no longer have to see Aaron Yoder's big, dirty footprint on her new book—the one he had stepped on, back on the first day of school.

Monday was still five whole days away! Lily felt almost too excited to eat. Not quite, but almost.

On Monday morning, Lily and Joseph didn't bother to wait for Hannah and Levi. They were too excited to see the new schoolhouse.

All of the other students felt the same way—they all arrived early. Everyone was excited to smell that fresh paint smell and be the first to walk on the new wooden floors. Beth and her brother Reuben arrived at school just as Lily and Joseph were about to enter the schoolhouse. "Wait, Lily! Wait for me. Let's go in together!" Beth ran up to the door.

Joseph went in but Lily paused by the door to wait for Beth. They held hands and walked over the threshold, barely able to hold their excitement in. It was beautiful! The walls had been painted a soft cream color. Shelves were built along the two sidewalls that went up to Lily's waist. The shelves were already filled with library books to read when they had spare time, and new board games and puzzles to play with at recess on rainy days. Farther down were encyclopedias, dictionaries, and stacks of songbooks.

The floor was painted a bluish gray. Lily checked her shoes

to make sure they weren't dirty before stepping off the rug and onto this pretty floor. She and Beth went to find their desks. They were still in the same places they had been, which was a little disappointing. Lily had hoped Teacher Rhoda might have moved Aaron Yoder's desk far, far away. No such luck. Maybe, if everything was clean and shiny and a fresh start, Aaron would start over with Lily, being nice and kind and sweet. She doubted it, but she hoped.

She opened the lid on her desk and paged through the new books inside.

Beth squealed. "Oh Lily, come look at this!"

Beth stood at the back of the room beside the little sink where everyone could wash their hands. Lily crossed the room to see what Beth was so excited about: beside the sink was a shiny new water fountain. It had a little handle to pull at the side, sending up an arching stream of cold water. Lily had never seen anything so wonderful. Beth held the strings of her covering to keep them from getting wet as she took a drink. Then Lily got a turn. They wouldn't have to share a water cup at the pump in the school yard. They wouldn't even have to go outside to have a drink. For the first time, Lily felt a little glad about that fire. New things were so much fun.

Teacher Rhoda rang the bell and everyone found their seats. As she read a Bible story, Lily sighed happily. It felt good to be back in school with the other children. Everything looked and smelled new and fresh and pretty. She couldn't wait to work in her new books with her new pencil and read all the new library books that were waiting on the bookshelves.

But there was even better news! Last night, Papa had told her he would buy a new box of sixty-four crayons for her the next time he went to town.

Mama's Pig Story

On the way back from the mailbox, Lily leafed through a magazine that had come in the mail today. Most of it was advertisements and a few articles about farming. Then a headline on a page caught her eye: "Submit your humorous story and win!" She read on: If the magazine printed your story, it would pay you one hundred dollars.

Lily tried to think of everything she could buy with one hundred dollars. Wouldn't Papa and Mama be pleased if she were paid for something she wrote? She was sure she could write a funny story. How easy! Simple. Funny things happened to her all the time. Practically every day.

Lily ran to her room and sat down at her desk with her writing tablet. Think, think, think. She tapped her pencil on her desktop. Then she drew a whole row of smiley faces along the top of her page and some flowers along the bottom. She noticed a dead bee on the windowsill and wondered how long it had been there. Think, think, think. What was something funny that had happened recently? Her mind was a blank.

She thought of dessert last night. Paul was eating the frosting off the cake top. When Papa told him to eat the bottom first, he turned his piece of cake upside down and kept eating the frosting. That was funny! Everyone laughed. But when Lily tried to write it, the story didn't seem very amusing. Who wanted to read about a baby?

She picked up the magazine and went to find Mama, hoping she might have a good idea for a funny story.

Mama skimmed the article. "I'm not sure what you could write about," she said. "Maybe you can make something up." She turned back to the article to read it more thoroughly. "Lily, would you mind if I tried writing a story too?"

"I don't mind," Lily said. Not a bit. She would be pleased if Mama had a story published in that magazine.

That evening, as soon as Paul was tucked into bed, Mama set to work. Lily watched her at the kitchen table. Her pencil flew back and forth across the paper. Lily's pencil never flew. It barely walked. Mama made it look so easy. Before long, she put her pencil down, satisfied. She handed the paper to Papa.

He read it and laughed out loud. "You did a fine job, Rachel."

Mama seemed pleased at Papa's praise. She let Lily read what she'd written. It was a story about the time Mama had helped catch a pig that had escaped from its pen. It was a very funny story and it was true.

Mama took a long envelope from Papa's desk and tucked her folded story inside. She addressed it in her neat, careful handwriting, stamped it, and propped it on top of the desk to take to the mailbox in the morning.

Lily looked at it. The envelope looked fat and interesting.

She hoped whoever read the story would like it as much as she and Papa had. She was sure that Mama would hear back from the publisher soon. So each day, she came home from school and asked Mama if she had heard from the magazine yet. Each day, Mama would smile and say not yet.

Then Lily forgot about it.

⚬⚬⚬

Weeks later, Mama met her at the door and held up an envelope for Lily to see. "They liked my story," she said. "I got a letter in the mail today saying they want to publish it in their next issue."

"Did they pay you one hundred dollars?" Lily asked. A fortune!

"Yes," Mama said. "And I already know how I want to spend it."

Lily did too! Candy, books, games.

"I want to buy a little coal water heater," Mama said.

What?! But, but, but . . . it should be spent on something fun! Lily thought. Something wonderful and delicious.

Mama smiled at the look of horror on Lily's face. "Wouldn't it be nice to not have to heat water on the stove to wash the dishes? Or in the big kettle in the basement for the laundry and bath time?"

Lily had to give that some thought. It would be nice to have hot water come straight out of the faucet. Not quite as nice as one hundred dollars' worth of candy, but it would be nice. "Does Papa know they liked your story?"

"Yes," Mama said. "He brought the mail to the house and watched me open the envelope. He already went to buy everything we need to set up the hot water heater."

Lily stopped to listen. No hum of Papa's woodworking machinery came from his shop. The house seemed strangely quiet.

Lily's excitement grew as she ran to change into her everyday clothes. She hoped Papa would get right to work on installing the coal water heater the minute he returned home. Papa knew how to do everything. Tonight, she might get to have a hot bath, with hot water right from the faucets!

When Papa returned from town, he started to cut copper pipes and fastened fittings to them. He installed the hot water pipes beside the cold water pipes that carried water throughout the house. He stopped only for supper, then lit the lantern and kept on working.

Too soon, it was time for bed. Papa hadn't finished and Lily was disappointed that she had to go to bed before there was running hot water. What about the hot bath she had planned? "Patience is needed in all kinds of things, Lily," Papa told her. "Including plumbing hardware. The glue on the pipes needs to dry overnight before we fire up the water heater. We don't want to have leaks just because we didn't wait long enough for everything to dry properly."

The next morning, Lily woke as the first streaks of pink tinted the eastern skies. She hopped out of bed, dressed quickly, and ran downstairs to the kitchen. Mama was making breakfast. Papa had already milked Pansy and was ready to start the fire in the water heater. He smiled when he saw Lily. "Would you run to the shop and bring back some wood shavings?"

Lily slipped on her coat and ran to Papa's shop. She filled

her apron with shavings from the pile under the wood planer. Down in the basement, Papa scooped several handfuls of shavings from her apron and piled them on top of wood scraps he had arranged on the bottom of the heater. He took a match and lit a piece of wood shaving. Lily and Papa and Mama watched as the flame flickered slowly, slowly, then poof! A fire started. Papa added a few scoopfuls of coal and closed the little door to the heater. "There," he said, satisfied. "If all goes according to plan, we should have hot water to wash the dishes by the time we're done eating breakfast."

"Can I wash dishes this morning all by myself?" Lily asked. She wanted to be the first one in the house to use the hot water.

Papa and Mama exchanged a look, then they both laughed. What was so funny?

"I don't think I've ever heard you volunteer to wash dishes," Mama said.

The very second Papa finished the prayer that signaled breakfast was over, Lily grabbed her plate and hurried over to the sink. She knew Joseph had his eye on that hot water faucet and wanted to be the first to try it. He had been talking about it all during breakfast. She opened the faucet and soon steamy hot water came pouring out. This was fun! She added soap and watched it bubble up. A nice layer of suds emerged on the top of the water—she didn't even have to swish her hands back and forth. Soon, the dishpan was full and she had to turn the water off. And then reality set in. The actual washing part was no different.

Lily looked at the mountain of dirty dishes and pans stacked on the counter. So that was why Papa and Mama had laughed. They knew that washing dishes was the same, no matter how the water had been heated. Her excitement about washing dishes fizzled out.

The next day was Sunday. Lily stood quietly next to Mama as the women visited with each other before church started. That's what little girls did until they turned ten and could visit with their friends. Alice Raber, Beth's mother, turned to Mama. "I read that story you wrote for that farm magazine. Jonas and I got a good laugh over it. Did it really happen that way?"

"Yes, it did," Mama said, chuckling. "It was a pig chase I'll never forget."

Other women had read the story and told Mama they enjoyed it. Everyone thought it was funny—everyone except for Ida Kauffman. Ida lifted her chin and looked down her nose at Lily, standing next to Mama. "Now I see why Lily is the way she is. Der Appel rollt net weit vum Baum." *The apple will not roll far away from its tree.*

How mean! How rude. Lily clenched her fists at her sides. Ida Kauffman was *just* like Effie. They both said hateful things. Lily thought about stepping on Ida's foot, hard, but Mama put a firm hand on her shoulder. "Well, Ida," Mama said in a sweet voice, "that pig chase story has provided us with money for hot water."

Ida Kauffman was flustered; she was at a rare loss for words. The Kauffmans didn't have hot water. Mama knew that! Lily could barely hold back a big grin. She did, she held back that smug grin, but just barely.

Mama's Pig Story

On a hot summer afternoon in July, our neighbor came huffing and puffing up our driveway, shouting, "Rachel! Rachel Lapp! Your pig got loose!"

My husband, Daniel, and I had been married only a few months. My uncle had given us a feeder pig as a wedding present. If we could get this pig up to a certain weight by winter, we would be able to sell it for a profit. But this pig was a little too smart for us. He escaped on a regular basis and found his way over to our neighbor's garden where he would root out carrots and potatoes, then roll in the soft, cool dirt.

Daniel tried all kinds of ways to keep that pig in his pen. Finally, he fenced the pen with chicken wire and put double latches on the gates. But obviously, that sneaky pig had found a way out of his pen and made his way into the neighbor's garden.

Our neighbor was a bachelor and liked to keep to himself. He was also a rather portly fellow. Chasing our pig off his property had quickly grown tiresome. Our friendship with our neighbor was on thin ice because of that clever pig.

On that July day, when I heard the neighbor call my name, I dashed outside and ran to the garden. There was the pig, rolling in mud in the neighbor's garden. Daniel was at work, so the task of retrieving the pig fell to me.

Most of you know that chasing a pig is no Sunday picnic. They are extremely difficult to catch. The neighbor quickly became winded and leaned against the fence to catch his breath. The pig darted and dashed all around the garden; I darted and dashed behind him. I was covered in mud, head to toe. But I refused to let that pig get the best of me. Finally, he paused by the zucchini plants to nibble some blossoms. I tiptoed up behind him and made a headlong dive. I caught him by the tail! He squealed and grunted as I slipped a rope around its neck. I had caught that smart pig all by myself! I couldn't wait to tell Daniel what I had done today.

I apologized to the neighbor and promised that Daniel would repair the damage done to the garden. I walked home with the pig, pleased. We were both covered in mud. I was grinning ear to ear, the pig was complaining. He kept up a steady stream of squeals, grunts, and grumbles.

Then an odd feeling started in my stomach and traveled to my head. Our feeder pig didn't have a tail. Sure enough, as I walked past the barn to the pigpen, there was our feeder pig, curled up in a corner of the pen, sound asleep.

I looked down at the pig by my side. "Oh my. You're not my pig."

He looked back up at me, as if to say, "That's what I was trying to tell you!"

CHAPTER

26

Holey Lily

Rain, rain, rain. It had rained so much the last few weeks that Lily had almost forgotten what a sunny day felt like. Today, though, the sun had broken through the lead gray clouds. Lily looked longingly out the schoolhouse window, eager to get outside and feel warm sunshine on her face.

"Put your books away for recess," Teacher Rhoda said.

Lily shoved her books inside her desk and stood, waiting to be dismissed. During noon recess, the children had played an exciting game of Prisoners' Base. Teacher Rhoda had rung the bell before they had time to finish and Lily couldn't wait to continue the game.

Everyone grabbed their coats from the hooks at the back of the schoolroom and got their boots on. The playground was still a little muddy from the rain they'd had earlier in the week.

Lily slipped her foot into her boot, but something felt strange. She pulled the boot off and found her shoe was covered with mud. She turned the boot upside down and poured the mud out. She looked into her other boot. Same thing. Filled with mud.

Aaron Yoder was watching her. He nudged Sam Stoltzfus with his elbow and pointed to Lily. The two of them doubled over with laughter. Lily would have liked to throw handfuls of mud right at their goofy faces, but then she would be in trouble. She'd had enough trouble lately.

Lily took her boots into the schoolhouse and poured water into them to try to wash the mud out. She tried to dry the insides with paper towels but it didn't work. Too soggy.

Teacher Rhoda helped her clean off her muddy shoe. "I think you should find something to play indoors until your boots have a chance to dry."

Lily was so angry! Aaron was the worst human being on earth—as bad as Effie. And now he had ruined an all-too-rare sunny day of recess.

It started as a small loose thread on the elbow of Lily's black sweater. It was just one thread, but she couldn't leave it alone. During silent reading periods in school, she would hold her elbows and twirl that thread ever so slightly, between her thumb and finger. Twist and twirl, twist and twirl. She thought about knotting it and breaking it off, but never quite got around to it. Her hands just naturally went to that tiny, out-of-place piece of loose yarn.

A few days later, during lunch recess, Effie pointed at Lily's elbow. "You have a great big hole!" Lily held out her arm to see what Effie was pointing to. She hadn't realized that the yarn had been unraveling as she twisted the thread. Her elbow was now sticking out of a gaping hole. Her beautiful sweater, new last Christmas!

Then Aaron noticed. He started chanting, "Holey Lily!" and Sam whooped with laughter. Soon half of the boys, along with Effie, were making fun of her sweater. That nickname worried her, too. Anytime Aaron gave someone a nickname, it stuck like flypaper.

When Lily got home from school, she showed Mama the hole in her sweater. She might have mentioned how annoying Effie was. And why did Effie have to point it out in front of everybody? Lily might have made the tiniest suggestion that Aaron Yoder should be sent to the moon.

Mama reserved judgment. She examined the sweater in the light by the window. "This hole reminds me of what happens when we don't forgive someone. Choosing to think about or gossip about someone who offends us is like twisting that tiny thread around between our fingers. It won't be long before that little thread causes a festering hole."

Effie, she meant. And Aaron.

Mama took out her darning needle and threaded it with black yarn. "You know, Lily, friendships aren't always easy, aren't always perfect, aren't always free from hurt. But it isn't right to just ignore people or wish they would be sent off someplace far, far away. How we choose to handle those times when we're wounded by a friend will make the difference between growing love or creating a hole."

Then she handed Lily the needle and yarn. "It's yours to fix."

Lily stared at the needle. A hole in a sweater was much easier to fix than Aaron Yoder and Effie Kauffman.

Levi Up a Tree

It was a rainy, blustery day and the children had to play indoors at recess in the basement. Lily and her friends jumped rope but the boys couldn't decide on anything. They were tossing around ideas. "If it wasn't raining it would be good weather to fly a kite," Levi said.

"But it is raining," Aaron Yoder pointed out with a sneer. "Hey, I've got an idea. Why don't we build kites that we could fly once it stops raining?"

The boys rallied behind that idea. Ezra Yoder started to give out instructions. He took some of the kindling and made wooden strips. He told two boys to run upstairs to ask Teacher Rhoda for some plastic shopping bags and needle and thread.

"Hold on!" Levi said. "I don't sew. That's girl work."

"Come on, Levi," Ezra said. "We always sew our own kites at home."

"Not me," Levi said. He turned to his sister. "Hannah, we need you and the other girls to sew our kites."

Hannah immediately dropped her end of the jump rope and it tangled up around Lily's feet. She bent down to untangle it while the other girls hurried over to start sewing kites for the boys.

How ridiculous! Just because the boys snapped their fingers, the silly girls jumped. Lily was disappointed. She hated to sew by hand, and she especially did not want to sew for any boy. Maybe she would help Joseph. But no other boys, not even Cousin Levi.

But jumping rope alone wasn't much fun. Finally, she moseyed over to where the girls were gathered. Ezra had tied kindling strips firmly together with baling twine and the girls set to work to try to sew the plastic bags over them. It was frustrating work for Lily. She tried to make the plastic bag taut around the tied kindling strips but it kept slipping out of place when she jabbed her needle into it. Even the older girls seemed to be having a hard time doing it, but they didn't seem to mind like Lily did. They talked and giggled at dumb things the boys said. Lily was disgusted. She thought the boys should make their own stupid kites. They were the ones who wanted them in the first place.

When Teacher Rhoda rang the bell, Lily dropped the kite she had been working on, happy to go to her desk and face math. Even studying percentages in arithmetic was better than hand sewing a plastic bag.

The next day was perfect kite weather. The sun shone and the wind whipped through the trees. The boys were eager to try out their new kites. They spent the first recess putting finishing touches on them, including tails made from an old sheet. By lunchtime, they were ready to try them out.

"I have the best kite," Levi said in his loud, look-at-me voice.

Aaron rolled his eyes. "We haven't even tried them out yet. We won't know who has the best until we see how they fly."

The girls watched as the boys held their kites and started to run, then let them go. Most of them nosedived into the ground behind them instead of lifting in the air and flying like a kite was supposed to do. Levi's kite, though, picked up the wind and started to drift higher and higher. Levi ran along under it, carefully releasing more and more string. The kite rose up and up, only to tangle in the branches of an oak tree at the edge of the school yard.

Levi ran to the tree, grabbed a low branch and hitched himself up on it. Then he started to climb, branch by branch.

Ezra cupped his hands around his mouth and shouted up to him. "Levi, you can't get that kite down. It's too high."

Levi looked down at Ezra and the other children who were gathering at the base of the tree, watching him. "Maybe for you, but I can easily get to it. I'm the best tree climber in the school."

Lily just knew this was a bad idea. She held her breath as she watched Levi climb higher and higher. He loved an audience and now he had one. He would never come down until he got that kite. All the other children stood with heads craned back, watching him with bated breath, waiting to see if he might fall. No one cared about the kites anymore. They wanted to see if Levi could climb to the top of the tree.

From the steps of the schoolhouse, Teacher Rhoda called

out, "Levi! I want you to come down right away. That kite isn't worth breaking your neck!"

But did Levi listen to her? No. He kept on climbing. The higher he climbed, the smaller the branches. Finally, Levi reached the top of the tree, close to the kite. It was caught on the tip of one of the branches. He inched his way out toward it. Nobody moved, nobody spoke, nobody breathed. Lily thought she heard a creaking sound. Levi reached his hand out to grab the kite and *SNAP!* The little branch he was hanging onto broke loose.

It seemed as if Levi fell in slow motion. His arms and legs flailed and he began to scream—a sound Lily would never forget. She squeezed her eyes shut and held her hands over her ears. She couldn't bear to watch. Then there was an awful thud as he hit the ground—so awful that even her hands over her ears couldn't muffle the sound. She opened her eyes to see Levi crumpled in a heap on the ground.

"He's dead!" Effie screamed. Then Hannah started to wail and all the other girls started crying with her. Sympathy criers.

Teacher Rhoda ran over to Levi. He wasn't moving. His eyes were closed. His legs were twisted at odd angles. Maybe Effie was right. He did seem surely dead. Teacher Rhoda looked up at Ezra. "Go to Ben Stoltzfus across the road and tell him we need to take Levi to the hospital right away."

Ezra Yoder ran to get help. Teacher Rhoda sat on the ground and spoke in a gentle voice to Levi. Lily patted Hannah's back. She didn't know what to say or to do about poor, dead Levi. Then Levi started to moan, which was a great relief. He wasn't quite as dead as everyone had thought.

Minutes that seemed like hours went by before Ezra returned with Ben Stoltzfus. "Try to hold still, Levi," Ben said when Levi's eyes flickered open. "I called one of your neighbors to bring your parents to school. They should be here soon."

A big station wagon drove into the school yard and Uncle Elmer jumped out of the passenger side. Uncle Elmer ran over to Levi and asked him where it hurt.

"Everywhere," Levi said to his father. "But my legs hurt the worst."

"I think we need to call an ambulance. I don't want to risk lifting you and hurting you even more." Uncle Elmer went over to speak to Mr. Beal, the neighbor who'd driven the station wagon.

Mr. Beal drove Ben Stoltzfus to the phone shanty to call an ambulance while Uncle Elmer stayed with Levi.

Teacher Rhoda let the children stay outside until the ambulance came. Then she shooed everyone out of the way. Two men in uniforms gently slipped a stretcher under Levi and lifted him into the back of the ambulance. Uncle Elmer climbed in and they headed to the hospital.

The students couldn't concentrate on their lessons for the rest of the day so Teacher Rhoda let everyone read silently at their desk. She seemed worried, too. Poor Levi.

Both of Levi's legs had been broken, badly. He was in a wheelchair and wouldn't be able to return to school for quite some time. Each evening, Teacher Rhoda packed up schoolwork and sent it home with Hannah so Levi could keep up.

Recess seemed strange without Levi and his endless bragging. Actually, it was nice! Whenever Lily thought about the difference Levi's absence made on the school yard, she felt little pinches of guilt. She should be feeling sad for his broken legs, not glad he wasn't at school. She *should*—but sometimes it was hard to tell your feelings to behave.

On Friday afternoon, Teacher Rhoda handed out blank sheets of sturdy paper. "I want each one of you to make a scrapbook sheet for Levi. You can draw pictures, write poems or riddles, stories, or anything you think he might enjoy seeing. Next week, we'll walk over to visit him and bring him the scrapbook."

Lily set right to work. She liked to draw flowers, but Levi

was a boy. He wouldn't appreciate her flowers. She thought of riddles, but he had heard most of them. Finally, she drew a few trees. At their base, she drew a little pile of logs with flames on them. Levi liked campfires.

When the students had finished, Teacher Rhoda made a cover to hold all the pages together, like a real book. On the front, she wrote "Get Well Soon" in her beautiful cursive handwriting.

On Monday afternoon, as soon as lunch was over, Teacher Rhoda announced that it was time to visit Levi. She asked Ezra Yoder to lead the way. She had the children walk single file behind Ezra, lined up by age, and then she followed at the end of the line. Lily thought it looked like the Canada geese in Uncle Elmer's pond. They walked single file with the Papa Goose in front and the Mama Goose at the end and all the baby goslings safely in between. Lily felt like quacking loudly but with Effie right in front of her, she decided not to. She would be scolded for not acting ladylike.

Levi was happy to have company. Aunt Mary hurried to prepare cookies and milk for everyone. Teacher Rhoda lined the students up on the front yard. They were going to sing two songs, Levi's favorites.

After they sang and ate their snack, it was time to present the scrapbook to Levi. Teacher Rhoda handed it to him and said, "We all miss you in school."

That was very nice of Teacher Rhoda to say, even though no one really did miss him. Ouch! Lily felt another prick of guilt, as real as a pin jab.

Levi looked through the book, pleased. Then Teacher Rhoda herded everyone together to walk back to school.

"Time to pretend we're baby geese again," Lily muttered to Hannah.

Lavina Schrock, a second grader, overheard her. She told her friends and soon the younger children started quacking. "Quack, quack!" More and more children joined in. "Quack, quack, quack!" Lily helped too and soon everyone was walking and quacking all the way back to school, even the big boys. Teacher Rhoda couldn't stop grinning.

For Levi's sake, Lily did hope that his legs would mend soon so that he could return to school. But that would mean he'd be back to the school yard with his tiresome one-upmanship.

Ouch! Another prick.

Still, the quacking line had been fun. It had been the best part of the day.

Lily Turns Ten

On a rainy afternoon, Mama spread several yards of fabric on the kitchen table. Lily watched as she placed patterns on top of it and carefully cut all the way around them.

Lily's birthday was just a few weeks away, and Mama was making new clothes for Lily. New clothes fit for a ten-year-old. Turning ten was the most important birthday in an Amish girl's life, and Lily could hardly wait. She would no longer wear loose-fitting dresses with buttons down the back. She would never wear a full-length apron again. Finally, she would be old enough to wear a dress that pinned in the front. Her dress would have a cape and apron. Becoming a grown-up was something Lily longed for. She was sure she would feel much, much older, more mature and ladylike, once she no longer had to wear dumb little-girl dresses.

Mama took the fabric pieces she had cut and sat down at her treadle sewing machine. Lily watched happily as her new dress took shape. As soon as Mama had finished sewing the seams, Lily tried it on. She stood quietly while Mama measured the skirt and pinned the bottom for the hem. She felt so strange in this new style of dress. Strange and wonderful. A wonderful kind of strange.

As soon as the cape and apron were sewn, Mama had Lily try them on and helped her stick the pins into the fabric to hold it all together. Lily had watched Mama put pins in her dress. It looked easy. But when she tried to do it, she poked herself. When she finally got some pins in, they were crooked. This was harder than it looked. Mama smiled and helped straighten out the pins. When the last pin was put in place, Lily ran to find a mirror.

Why . . . she did look different! Lily felt so grown-up with a cape around her shoulders and an apron belt pinned snugly at her waist. Mama came up behind Lily in the mirror, her eyes softening at the sight. Lily was sure she knew what was running through Mama's mind: *How sad that I only have one little girl. And so many boys.*

Then the moment passed and Mama was back to business. "After you change into your everyday dress, you can go play with your brothers. I'm going to try and get one more dress sewn while Paul is napping."

As Lily unpinned her lovely new dress, she wondered how she could possibly wait to wear it until her birthday.

Lily jumped out of bed the minute she heard Mama's soft footsteps in the kitchen. Today was her birthday. Today she was ten years old! She dressed and ran downstairs. She didn't want to miss a single moment of this special day.

Mama smiled when she saw Lily at the door. "Good morning!" She gave Lily a quick hug and said, "Happy birthday, my little lady."

Up until today, Mama had called her "my little girl." Lily grinned. "Little lady" sounded so much more grown-up than "little girl."

Lily set the table and made sure she put the special birthday plate at her place. Even better than the plate was that she wouldn't have to eat porridge today. Mama had bought a box of cornflakes for a special treat and Lily could hardly wait to pour them in a bowl and eat them.

Papa came in the kitchen door from the barn and set the pail of Pansy's milk on the floor beside the sink. He gently pinched Lily's cheek and said, "Happy birthday, Lily."

During breakfast, Lily made sure that Joseph and Dannie knew how much she was enjoying her cornflakes. She'd nearly finished her second bowl and was considering a third. "Can I wear my new dress to school today?" she asked between spoonfuls.

"Not yet," Mama said. "You can wear it to go to church next Sunday when you sit with the other girls."

Lily pondered Mama's comment as she poured her third bowl of cornflakes. She was disappointed to have to wait to wear her new dress. But she was happy to think about sitting with the girls for church. Cousin Hannah, Beth, and Effie had already turned ten and had been sitting with the girls instead of with their mothers. Finally, Lily could join them. She felt a pinch of pity for Malinda, whose birthday wouldn't come until summer. Just a pinch, though. Mostly, she was glad she wasn't the youngest girl.

"I want you to hurry home right after school today," Mama

told Lily as she and Joseph picked up their lunch boxes for school. Mama didn't explain why, but Lily hoped that meant there was going to be a birthday celebration tonight.

All day, Lily had a hard time concentrating on her school lessons. She kept thinking about the new dress, just waiting to be worn. Her mind drifted off to wonder what gifts Papa and Mama would give her this year. Since she was practically a grown-up, she was sure the gifts would be grown-up, too. Like a box of crayons with hundreds of colors. Was there such a thing? She hoped so.

As soon as Teacher Rhoda dismissed school for the day, Lily grabbed her lunch box and started running up the road. She didn't even wait to say goodbye to her friends. Not today. There would be no dawdling to look at flowers or watching the water run in the little stream beside the road. She was too excited.

Lily burst into the kitchen and found Grandma Miller and Aunt Susie hard at work, helping Mama. Grandma decorated a cake while Aunt Susie peeled potatoes. Dannie stood on a chair next to Grandma. Lily saw him swipe bits of frosting whenever he thought she wasn't looking.

"Happy birthday, Lily," Grandma and Aunt Susie said at the same time, as if they had rehearsed it.

Aunt Susie's brow wrinkled in a frown. "Where is Joseph?" She was a worrier.

"He was too slow today," Lily said. "I ran all the way home without him. He'll be here soon."

As if on cue, the door banged and Joseph blew into the kitchen. Right on his heels was Cousin Hannah. "Lily, why didn't you wait for us?" Hannah asked.

"I didn't know you were going to come home with me today," Lily said.

"It was going to be a surprise," Hannah said. "I was going to walk all the way home with you but you were running too fast. I couldn't even catch up with you." She looked and sounded very disappointed.

Not fair! How could Lily have known? Just as she braced herself to prepare for Mama's scolding about running ahead, she saw a slight smile on Mama's face. She understood! She realized how important it was to turn ten.

It wasn't long before other relatives started to arrive. The Lapp home was a jumble of noise and happiness. Lily liked all the chatter and laughter that filled the house as the women visited with each other while preparing supper. Papa stopped his day's work early and sat in the living room to talk with the men. The children played with the toys in the toy box in the corner of the kitchen.

Delicious smells filled the air and soon Mama called everyone to gather at the table. Mama had made all of Lily's favorite foods: fried chicken, fluffy mashed potatoes topped with browned butter and sprinkled with parsley, fried green beans with bacon bits, and golden flaky biscuits. Lily would be served first tonight because it was her birthday. She gazed around the table at the faces she loved and felt so happy.

Mama cut the chocolate birthday cake while Aunt Mary went down to the basement and came back with boxes of vanilla ice cream. A special treat! As soon as the cake and ice cream were eaten, Mama placed a big package and a small package in front of Lily. "Happy birthday," she said.

First, Lily opened the big package. It was a new black sweater to wear to school. The schoolhouse could be cold during spring, when Teacher Rhoda didn't always use the coal heater. She put the sweater on and spun around. "Thank you, Mama."

Lily opened the little package and found a cute heart-shaped ceramic dish with a lid. "You'll need something to keep your pins in since you will be wearing new dresses," Mama said.

How pretty it would look on top of the dresser in Lily's room. How grown-up!

"There's something else in the box," Mama said.

At the bottom of the box, Lily found a small stack of envelopes and a booklet of stamps.

Mama smiled. "You are old enough now to have your own circle letter."

Oh my. Oh my goodness! Lily was delighted. Mama had many circle letters and Lily had wanted one of her own for a long time. She would write her first letter tonight after everyone had gone home.

But first . . . there were more presents to come.

Grandma handed Lily an envelope. Inside was a birthday card, and inside of that was a crisp twenty-dollar bill. It fell onto her lap. She gasped and picked it up. She felt rich! She had never before, not in her entire life, had a twenty-dollar bill of her own. She'd never even held one in her hands!

"I wanted to buy fabric for your mother to make a new dress for you," Grandma said. "But I didn't get to town this week. I decided you might like to choose your own fabric if I gave you money to buy it."

Imagine that! Lily would go to the fabric shop and choose the material for a dress, all by herself. Just like Mama! She knew she would choose a purple fabric. "Oh, thank you, Grandma," Lily said.

Uncle Elmer and Aunt Mary gave Lily a new book, *The Mystifying Twins*. Lily turned it over and read the back cover copy: "Twin sisters pretend to be each other and end up in a lot of mischief." She was happy to have another book to add to her growing collection. On the inside cover, Aunt Mary had written in her very excellent cursive handwriting that only Lily could read (because Joseph wasn't old enough to read cursive):

To our Lily with our love, Aunt Mary and Uncle Elmer, Levi, Hannah, and Davy

Uncle Jacob started to chuckle. "I'm not sure if I should give you our present," he said as he handed Lily a small paper bag.

Lily opened it and drew out a book, *The Mystifying Twins.* The very same book! Of all the books in the world, it was amazing to think both aunts had bought her the same book.

"It must be a really good book if you need two copies of it," Papa said.

"I can get you a different book," Aunt Lizzie said.

Lily read the inscription inside the front cover. Aunt Lizzie had nice handwriting too. Not quite as fancy as Aunt Mary's, but close.

To Lily, From Uncle Jacob and Aunt Lizzie on your tenth birthday

At the bottom, Aunt Lizzie had penned a little poem:

When the sun of life is setting
And your hair is turning gray
May you be the same sweet lady
As the girl you are today.

Lily looked up. "If you don't mind, I'd like to keep them both." These inscriptions were much too special to give up.

"You're welcome to keep it," Uncle Jacob said, "if you're sure you want two of the same book."

"I'm sure," Lily said. She was absolutely, positively sure.

Her last gift came from Joseph and Dannie. They handed her a piece of paper that said: "We got you two gifts. One, we'll wash dishes for a week. Two, we'll dry dishes for a week."

"But will it be the same week?" Uncle Elmer asked and everyone laughed.

The men went back into the living room to visit while the women cleared all the food and dirty dishes away. All but Lily. She wasn't expected to wash and dry dishes on her birthday. After the last dish was put away, Grandma looked at the clock and said, "Well, I think it's time to start for home."

Soon, the noisy house turned quiet again. The only sound Lily heard was the creak of Papa's rocking chair as he rocked Paul to sleep.

"Mama, can you help me get my circle letter started?" Lily asked.

Mama pulled out a chair at the kitchen table and sat down. "Yes, I have time right now. First, pick nine of your friends whom you want to include in the letter."

Lily had to think that over. "Definitely Beth and Cousin Hannah." Definitely *not* Effie Kauffman. Mandy Mast from New York came to mind, even though Mandy had been a sore trial to Lily. As sore a trial as Effie.

"That's a good start," Mama said. "It might be nice to add some of your cousins whom you don't know very well. It would give you a chance to get to know them better."

Mama helped Lily chose several girl cousins who were close in age. She had sixty-five cousins, but most were much older or much younger or were boys so they didn't count. Mama found all the addresses Lily would need and made an address sheet. Lily's name and address was the first one, then Mandy Mast's. One by one the other girls' names and addresses were added.

Lily wrote a newsy letter, tucked it into an envelope along with the address sheet and sealed it. Tomorrow she would put it in the mailbox. In a month or so, Mama said, she would get an envelope filled with letters to read. Just like Mama did. Then Lily would take out the letter she had written and start a new one to send on with all the other letters. It would make circle after circle, always bringing new letters to read from her friends.

Later, Lily snuggled deep under her covers. She would never forget this day. It was the best birthday she had ever had. After all, a little lady turned ten only once in her life.

Lily's New Blue Dress

After supper on Friday, Lily cleared the dishes off the table and took them to Mama at the sink. "I'm going to town tomorrow," Mama said. "I need to go to the fabric store and thought you might like to come along and choose a fabric for a dress from Grandma's birthday money."

Lily knew just what she would pick. Purple. Lily would like every dress she wore to be some variation of the color purple: lavender, amethyst, violet, orchid—all the colors of purple that were in her new box of sixty-four crayons.

"Where will the boys be while we are in town?" Lily hoped the boys would stay at Grandma and Grandpa Miller's. It would be much better to go fabric shopping without three little brothers tagging along.

"Papa will stay home with the boys," Mama said. "He called a driver to take us to town."

That was excellent news. Excellent. Going to town was

a rare treat. Driving in a car was even more special. Mama didn't like to drive Jim and the buggy to town, not unless Papa was with her. Lily could hardly wait until tomorrow.

The next morning, Lily and Mama hurried to try to get most of the Saturday cleaning done before the driver came. In between chores, Lily kept running to the window to see if a car had pulled into the driveway. At long last, she heard a crunchy sound on the gravel. This time, when she looked out the window she saw Mr. Tanner's big blue car.

"He's here!" Lily called to Mama. She ran to get her big black bonnet and slipped it on over her prayer covering. She tied it as neatly as she could and stood by the door to wait for Mama.

When Mama opened the back door of Mr. Tanner's car, Lily slid onto the seat. Mama sat beside her and closed the door.

"Where to?" Mr. Tanner asked.

"Cloverdale. First, the grocery store and then the fabric shop," Mama said.

Lily peered out the window as Mr. Tanner drove down the road. It felt as if the car was a boat, sailing on an ocean. Trees and fields whizzed past. Lily barely spotted a horse grazing in a pasture and *WHOOSH!* It was gone. She liked going fast and it meant they would get to the fabric shop much more quickly than with Jim—though she missed all the interesting things to notice from a buggy window. But then she unrolled the window and breathed in the fresh air. Not a whiff of horse anywhere! Her cap strings unraveled and danced in the wind. Lily decided she liked car travel best of all. Fast was fun.

The groceries were quickly purchased and soon they were

at the fabric shop. Lily had been there once before, with Papa last fall, and it still looked every bit as interesting. But this was different. This time, Mama would be buying Lily fabric for her grown-up dresses.

Mama walked to the aisle filled with bolts of solid colors of fabric. She drew out several bolts of blue and green fabrics and another one of black. She told the shopkeeper to cut four yards of each bolt.

Lily wandered up and down the aisle. If she squinted her eyes slightly, the colors blurred together and looked like a rainbow. Then her eyes popped open. There was the most beautiful aqua blue that she had ever seen. It almost shimmered, like a tropical sea. She stroked it. It felt soft and slippery and not like any dress she had ever had. "Look at this fabric, Mama," Lily said.

Mama came over and looked at it. "It is very pretty," she said. "But not very practical. It would probably snag easily. And shrink when I washed it. It's almost too bright."

How could anything be *too* bright? "Oh Mama, it's so pretty," Lily said. "I could save it to go to church. I would take care not to snag it."

But Mama was wavering, Lily could see that.

Mama fingered the fabric a little more. "Did you see the nice purple fabrics they have?"

"Yes, but I like this even better."

Mama sighed. "We can't get both of them. Are you sure you want this blue over any purple?"

Absolutely! "I'm sure." Lily had never been more sure of anything. This was the most beautiful fabric she had ever seen.

Mama drew the bolt of fabric out and placed it on the counter. "I'll take four yards of this too," she said. Lily

watched as the shopkeeper measured the fabric and cut it.
The pair of scissors slid effortlessly through the fabric, like
it was cutting butter. It even sounded different while it was
being cut than the other fabrics did.

After Mama had paid the shopkeeper for all the fabric,
they walked back to the car.

Mr. Tanner had been reading a book while he waited
and set it down when Mama and Lily climbed into the car.
"Where to?"

"Home," Mama said.

Lily was glad. She hoped Mama would start sewing her beautiful new dress as soon as they got home. She would even offer to help, though she didn't like to sew. She planned to wear this dress to church next Sunday—her very first church service as a ten-year-old.

As soon as the car pulled into the driveway, Lily didn't bother to wait for Mama to pay Mr. Tanner. She quickly ran to the house and spread her fabric out on the table. She found a big envelope in Mama's basket marked "Lily's dress pattern, age ten." She took Mama's good fabric scissors from the sewing table and set everything on the table so Mama could get right to work the minute she got into the house.

Mama's eyes opened wide in surprise when she came inside and saw the table. "I'm sorry, Lily," she said. "But that dress will have to wait a little while yet. I want to make a black dress for you first. It's always important to have a black dress ready to wear."

What? Lily was disappointed. She did not like to wear black. The only time she wore black was at communion or baptism services in church or when there was a funeral. All boring, boring, boring. Wearing black meant solemn occasions. Lily would rather feel light and happy, not sad or solemn.

A few days later, Lily came home from school and found her aquamarine fabric turned into a dress, waiting on her bed. It was so beautiful! Lily hung it carefully inside her closet and closed the door. No—that wouldn't do for such a lovely dress. It was a shame to hide a bright blue dress inside a closet. She opened the door and took out the dress to hang on a hook on the wall. She sat on the edge of her bed, admiring her choice. The beautiful aqua blue shimmered in the sunlight. She could hardly wait until Sunday.

She spent some time imagining the conversation that would go on about this dress. They would all admire it. Beth and Cousin Hannah would say they hoped their mothers would make one just like it and Effie would sniff and say she was glad she would never wear such a fancy color. Lily knew her well enough to know that was Effie's way of saying she wanted it.

Oh, Lily hoped nobody died before Sunday! How terrible it would be to have to wear black instead of this lovely dress.

Lily counted down the days until Sunday. Every time she heard a buggy on the road, she held her breath until it passed by. Then she knew it wasn't someone coming to visit with bad news about someone dying.

Finally, finally! Sunday morning arrived. Lily slipped into her new dress and Mama helped her with all the pins. Lily loved how the fabric felt. It was soft and slippery and made a swishing noise when she walked.

She sat like a statue on the buggy seat to make sure nothing happened to her dress before they got to church. Papa stopped in front of the house where church would be held. Ever so carefully, Lily climbed out of the back of the buggy and stood waiting until Mama got out with baby Paul in her arms. They walked into the house together to join the women and girls in the kitchen. Joseph and Dannie went with Papa to unhitch Jim. Then they would stand outside and visit with the rest of the men and boys until it was time for church to start.

All of Lily's friends oohed and aahed over her new blue

dress—all except Effie, of course. They pinched her arm lightly just like the big girls did whenever someone wore a new dress for the first time.

Lily followed Mama to shake all the women's and girls' hands. This time, instead of standing next to Mama while they waited until it was time to file to their seats, she went to stand with the girls. Everyone was visiting softly but for once Lily couldn't think of anything to say. It all seemed too strange. Not being with Mama. Wearing her new grown-up dress. She felt odd, like her tummy was doing somersaults.

Benches had been set up in the living room. The women filed in but Lily stood and waited with the rest of the girls until it was time for them to file in. The men came in next, then the girls lined up—oldest ones first.

Once again, Lily was the youngest. She stood at the very end of the line. They filed in front of the ministers and walked along the side of the room and sat on the benches behind the men. Lily's heart felt like it was thumping loudly in her chest—*Ba bump! Ba bump! Ba bump!* Surely everyone could hear it. It all seemed so strange, she almost wished she could turn back the clock a week and be nine years old, seated next to Mama again. But that would never happen. She was ten now. Practically all grown up.

The boys filed in last, oldest to youngest, and sat behind the girls. After everyone had a seat, the bishop cleared his throat and solemnly announced that it was time for church to begin. Always, always so solemn.

The song leader called out the page for the first song. Effie opened the hymnbook and shared it with Lily. Effie was acting very sweet, which Lily thought was a nice surprise for her birthday. Lily tried to hold still and sing but her new dress was beginning to feel uncomfortable. The apron belt felt pinned so firmly around her waist, like a tight cinch. When she moved too quickly, she felt pricked by the points of pins. How did her friends get used to this? She thought wistfully of her loose, comfortable little-girl dresses. Growing up wasn't quite as much fun as she thought it would be.

After church was over, Lily followed the other girls upstairs to sit and visit while the women prepared lunch. Malinda ran to join them. "Oh, Lily! There is something on your new dress!"

"Where?" Lily asked.

Malinda pointed to Lily's backside. "Where you sit."

Lily backed up to a mirror and peered over her shoulder to see what was on her dress. A big wad of gum! Her heart sank.

Lily reached back and tried to remove it but it was stuck firmly. Beth and Hannah came over to see what was wrong, but they didn't know what to do about it either. Effie seemed pleased and Lily wanted to smack her. Effie had been chewing a big wad of Bazooka bubble gum before church.

"I'll go get your mama," Hannah said. She disappeared down the stairs and a minute later she came back with Mama.

Mama looked at the wad of gum and shook her head. "It looks as if you have been sitting on it all morning," she said. She tried to pick some of it off but only a few little bits came off and the rest stayed stuck tight. "We'll have to wait until we get home to get it out."

Cousin Hannah offered to walk right behind Lily so nobody could see the gum when it was time to go eat.

Lily was glad when Mama came to say that it was time to go home. She was exhausted. This first day of wearing a grown-up outfit and sitting with the girls had been a huge disappointment.

As soon as they got home, Lily changed her clothes and took her new dress downstairs. "Today is Sunday," Mama reminded her when Lily asked her if they could remove the gum right away. "We can try to remove it tomorrow, but I'm afraid there will be a stain there even if I can remove the gum."

Oh no! Lily hadn't thought about a stain. Maybe if she prayed and asked God to make sure the gum would all come out nicely she wouldn't have to worry about it. She was worrying quite a bit about this dress.

When Lily came home from school on Monday, she found Mama at the sewing machine with Lily's dress. Lily was almost afraid of what Mama was doing. She wouldn't look. She wouldn't look. She looked.

Oh . . . no. A patch! Mama was sewing a patch on Lily's dress.

"I'm so sorry, Lily," Mama said. "When I tried to remove the gum, the fabric tore."

How awful! Tears welled up in Lily's eyes.

"You can still wear it for everyday," Mama said, a little too brightly. "I should have listened to my instincts and encouraged you to get a more practical fabric at the fabric shop. This can serve as a good lesson that we should think more carefully before we buy something."

Lily didn't think *that* was the lesson to learn. She thought the only lesson would be to look first and make sure there was no gum and no Effie anywhere before she sat down.

CHAPTER

30

Stuck in the Basement
with Aaron Yoder

On a Friday afternoon, Teacher Rhoda told the students to put away their books for recess. It was the first warm day of spring, and the sunshine was beckoning for the students to come play in it. Lily couldn't wait to run outside.

Instead, Teacher Rhoda made a terrible announcement. "It's time for some serious cleaning of the schoolhouse," she said cheerfully. Aaron Yoder groaned out loud. Sam Stoltzfus clunked his head against his desk.

Teacher Rhoda drew a box from her bottom drawer. It held little pieces of paper with all the cleaning chores written on them. One by one, the children walked up to her desk and drew a slip of paper out of the box. Lily was very disappointed that recess would be spent cleaning, but she hoped at the very least that she would get to dust the erasers or wash the blackboard. Those were her two favorite chores. Her least favorite was to mop the floor and her very least favorite was to clean the basement. She shuddered. Too many spiders in the basement.

Oh no! Lily's paper read "Clean the basement." She would have to sweep it, shake the rugs, and then dump buckets of water on the floor and sweep it down the drain. Awful!

Then came even worse news. Aaron Yoder drew the same assignment. He and Lily would have to work together in the basement. The happiness she had felt about this beautiful sunny day plunged. It was turning into a terrible day.

As soon as everyone had their assigned chores, the children got right to work. Some children swept the schoolhouse, while others waited to mop until they were done. Some washed windows and scrubbed down the shelves that held the lunch boxes. Feeling sorry for herself, Lily trudged down the stairs to join horrible Aaron and sweep the basement.

Silently, Aaron and Lily set to work. Lily swept as fast as she could, sweeping up a dust cloud in the air. Aaron held the dustpan for her while she swept the big dirt pile into it. Next it was time to wash the floor. They filled several buckets with water and swooshed it over the floor. They swished their brooms back and forth, back and forth, scrubbing as they went. It was a blur of motion, and they didn't talk to each other, didn't even look at each other. So far, so good.

As usual, Aaron had to ruin everything. "I'm going to make you topple right over." He started swishing the broom toward Lily's feet.

Lily did the best she could to try to ignore him. She kept moving her feet away from Aaron's broom, but then he hit her feet hard. She slipped on the wet floor and fell down hard, hitting her head as she fell. Lily lay flat on the floor, trying to catch her breath.

"Uh-oh. Are you dead?" Aaron peered down at her, looking scared. He dropped his broom and bolted up the basement stairs and out to the school yard.

She hated Aaron Yoder. He was the meanest person on this earth. She would never speak to him again. Never.

Teacher Rhoda came down to the basement and saw Lily, splayed out on the floor. "What happened?" she asked as she helped Lily to her feet. The back of Lily's dress was soaking wet.

In a teary, angry voice, Lily told Teacher Rhoda that Aaron had made her fall on purpose.

Aaron was peeping in at them through the window. When he saw that they noticed him, he ran away. Teacher Rhoda went to the door and opened it. "Aaron! Come in here." She turned to Lily. "You can go upstairs."

As Lily went upstairs, she hoped Teacher Rhoda would let Aaron have it. She hoped his parents would be called in and told that their son couldn't be in school anymore. He would be expelled. He deserved it!

Soon—too soon—Teacher Rhoda came up the stairs. She went to Lily and said in a low voice, "Go down to the basement. Aaron has something he wants to say to you."

No! Lily didn't want to hear anything from Aaron. She only wanted him to get in trouble. But it wouldn't be right to say such a thing to Teacher Rhoda. She walked back down to the basement—but slowly. Aaron sat next to the sandbox, scooping sand in his hand and letting it go. When he saw Lily, he rose to his feet. "I'm sorry I made you fall over." Then a tight look came over his face as he choked out the words, "And I'll try to be nicer to you from now on."

Lily wasn't sure how to respond. She didn't want to say that she forgave him because that would be a lie. She would never forgive the worst person on earth. She whispered a quiet and hostile "Fine!" and hurried back up the stairs to safety.

It was a good thing that her thoughts could stay private. What she was really thinking was, *I'll believe* that *when I see it, you awful, horrible boy.*

A Hurt Toe and an Escape from School

*I*t was warm, too warm to be wearing shoes. Lily wiggled her toes inside her shoes as she sat in the shade under a big maple tree with the rest of the girls one Sunday afternoon after church.

Turning ten meant grown-up dresses, and it also meant wearing shoes to church. Every time—even if it was a warm spring day. Lily had become accustomed to wearing the dresses and the snug apron belt no longer bothered her, but she didn't think she would ever get used to wearing shoes when the weather was warm.

She watched some of the little girls who ran around in their bare feet. She felt like telling them to run and jump and hop and enjoy being at church with bare feet before they turned ten and had to wear clunky, hot shoes, too.

Beth and Cousin Hannah were braiding a daisy chain. Effie was chattering away about everything she would do when she grew older. "I'm going to make Aaron Yoder come calling on me."

Lily was horrified. First, Cousin Hannah had an un-understandable crush on Aaron Yoder. Now Effie? Why did the girls think Aaron Yoder was so special? He wasn't!

Hannah did not like to hear Effie's plans for Aaron. "You can't *make* a boy come calling," Hannah said. "Boys decide who they want to go calling on. Girls don't ask boys."

"Oh, but I promised to marry Aaron when I was in first grade," Effie said. She smiled at Hannah, but her eyes weren't smiling.

Lily sighed. This conversation was ridiculous. Just ridiculous. The little girls ran past them again. They seemed so lighthearted and happy as their bare feet skimmed along the neatly mowed grass.

Lily made up her mind. She was going to help the little girls play tag. Anything was better than sitting under this tree listening to Effie's big plans for Aaron Yoder.

Quietly, she bent down, untied her shoes, and slipped them off. She rolled down her stockings and tucked them into the toes of her shoes to make sure she wouldn't lose them. Effie was watching. Her eyebrows shot up as Lily stood.

"You can't go barefoot in church now that you wear a cape and apron," Effie said.

Lily wiggled her toes in the grass. It felt so good! "But Effie," she said in her sugary-sweet voice, "church is over already."

Surprisingly, Effie didn't have a snappy retort. Lily ran to join the other little girls in their game. She was happy to leave her friends under the tree with their tiresome talk about boys. About Aaron.

The little girls were delighted to have a big girl join them. Soon, Lily was tagged *it*. She ran along a fence after Lavina, a little eight-year-old who was one of her favorites. Just as Lily reached out to touch Lavina, her big toe caught on a piece of wire and she fell flat on her face.

She sat up and tried to catch her breath. She looked down at her toe and squeezed her eyes shut. Her big toenail had been torn almost completely off and was now dangling by only one little corner. It hurt so much that she wanted to cry. She couldn't cry, though, not in front of the little girls. She hobbled gingerly back to the tree, picked her shoes up, and headed for the house to show Mama what had happened.

Mama took one look at it and had Lily sit down in a chair. Someone brought a Band-Aid. Mama reached down to Lily's toe and gave a quick jerk to remove the nail. She carefully washed her toe and bandaged it.

Lily sat beside Mama for the rest of the afternoon. Her toe throbbed painfully. It felt like it was on fire.

Listening to the women talk was even more painful. She heard Ida Kauffman whisper loudly to Alice, Beth's mother, "Lily Lapp is such a tomboy. If she were my daughter, I would turn her into a proper little girl in a hurry."

Lily cringed at the thought of being Ida's little girl. Imagine if she ended up just like Effie! *Two Effies!* Lily shuddered.

On Monday morning, Joseph stood at the blackboard, trying to figure out a long division problem. Teacher Rhoda patiently explained the process one more time, but Lily could see that Joseph didn't understand. He hated math and he especially hated long division.

At breakfast, Joseph had pretended to have a stomachache and said he didn't want to go to school. Mama said she was pretty sure his stomachache would disappear after math period. Lily never liked long division, either, but it seemed to be harder for Joseph to catch on to it than it was for her.

Teacher Rhoda tried again with Joseph, going over a few more problems slowly and carefully. She sent Joseph to his desk to complete the rest of the assignment on his own. He walked slowly to his desk, head hung low, and opened his books. Lily watched as he worked. His tongue escaped the side of his mouth as he labored. Soon, her attention turned back to the book she was reading.

Lily barely noticed that Teacher Rhoda gave Joseph permission to go to the bathroom. She turned around in her desk just in time to see her brother pause at the back of the schoolhouse. He grabbed his lunch box off the shelf and his straw hat off the hook. Then he bolted out the door.

Lily was shocked! What was Joseph doing?! Teacher Rhoda hurried to the door and called, "Joseph! Joseph!" But Joseph kept right on running as if his pants were on fire. All of the children ran to the windows to watch Joseph's escape. Aaron Yoder burst out laughing when Joseph disappeared over the hilltop.

Lily glared at Aaron. This wasn't funny! No one ever ran home from school during the day. Never! Joseph was going to be in big trouble.

Teacher Rhoda asked the third grade to turn in their arithmetic assignments and gave them new work. Soon everyone seemed to have forgotten about Joseph. All except Lily. She couldn't concentrate on anything. Her stomach felt achy for him.

Soon, Lily heard a horse and buggy trot down the road, then slow to a walk as it neared the schoolhouse. Through the window, Lily saw Papa tie Jim to the hitching post. He helped Joseph down and the two of them walked, hand in hand, back to the schoolhouse. Teacher Rhoda went outside to meet them. Lily strained her ears trying to hear what they were saying, but their voices were too soft. Then Joseph came inside, head hung low, and put away his lunch box. Teacher Rhoda asked Ezra Yoder to help Joseph with long division at the blackboard while she took care of some other classes. Lily saw Papa drive Jim back down the road.

That afternoon, Joseph waited until his friends had left for home before he started for home. He was in a bad mood all day, and Lily knew he didn't want to listen to any more teasing from his friends. She waited for him by the door. "What made you run away from school?"

Joseph scowled at her. "I kept getting the answers wrong! I tried and tried and tried. I told myself if I got it wrong one more time, I was going to run home. So when Teacher Rhoda said it was still wrong, I ran home."

"Didn't you hear her call to you?"

"Yes, but it was too late. I wanted to go home."

"What did Mama and Papa say?"

Joseph kicked at a stone on the road. "I didn't even get to eat a snack before Papa had Jim hitched up to take me back."

After supper that evening, Papa sat down to help Joseph learn how to do long division. Papa did his best, but Joseph was an exceptionally stubborn student. When Papa's frustration began to rise, Mama took a turn and tried to teach

Joseph. Lily thought she might be able to help, too, if Mama lost patience. She had never seen anyone so determined to not understand math.

It had been a long week. It started on Sunday with Lily's hurt toe—which still hurt. On Monday, there was Joseph's escape from school, which Aaron and Sam still teased him about. Then it rained for three straight days, which made the playground a boggy mess. Finally, Friday had come and with it, sunshine. Mama had a big smile on her face when Lily walked through the kitchen door after school. She pointed to the kitchen table. "Your circle letter has circled back to you, Lily!"

Lily sat right down and read through her letters. Then she started a new one, using her very finest cursive, of which she was secretly proud.

Dear friends and cousins,

Greetings of love sent to each of you as this pack of letters lands on your doorstep.

I was so happy to find this fat envelope waiting on the table for me when I came home from school. I read all your letters right away, even before I helped Mama get supper ready.

Today was a sunny day. It was warm enough that we could sit outside to eat our lunches. I like when we can do that, but today there was a pesky fly that kept bothering us. It kept sitting on Beth's sandwich while she was eating it.

Paul is getting so big. He likes being with me and he

likes best when I can make bubble juice on Saturday after the cleaning is done. He likes chasing bubbles when I blow them. He tries to catch them. He thinks they are balls and always looks surprised when they pop. It is so funny!

We only have a few more weeks of school left. I like school but I like summer, too. We will have a bigger garden this year. Mama says it takes more food since we are all getting bigger. We already planted all the early things and Papa wants to put up chicken fences for the peas next week before they get too big and topple over.

Well, that is all my important news for now.

Love,
Lily

Lily hurried to address her letter and put a stamp on the envelope. Then she ran outside and put it in the mailbox for tomorrow's pickup. The week, for Lily, had taken a very nice turn.

Love at First Splash

Church would be at Cousin Hannah's house today—close enough to walk. "Jim gets a Sabbath rest today, too," Papa had said as they walked down the lane after breakfast. Lily wondered if Jim really wanted a Sabbath rest. If she were a horse, she would want to see all her horse friends. It must be lonely for Jim to stay at home with no one except Pansy the cow, some annoying goats, and a couple of chickens to keep him company.

As they turned into Hannah's driveway, Lily forgot about Jim and thought about this afternoon—after the long, long, long church service and after lunch, when the girls could gather together and play. That was the best part of Sunday, the very best. Just thinking about it helped her be quiet and good during church.

A few hours later, as soon as lunch was finished, Lily and her friends had gathered in Cousin Hannah's bedroom to play. The girls were just deciding what to play when Mama knocked on the door and said, "Lily, we're going home."

What? How disappointing! But Lily knew she didn't have a say-so in the matter. She followed Mama downstairs. Papa put baby Paul in the little wagon and off they went down the driveway. Lily turned and looked back at Hannah's window, wondering which game her friends had chosen to play. It wasn't fair.

Then came even worse news. As soon as they reached home, Papa told the children to take a nap.

How awful! Lily didn't like taking a nap during the day. It was such a waste of time. And why would a ten-year-old have to take a nap? Naps were for babies and little boys, like Joseph and Dannie and Paul. Not for nearly grown-up girls.

As if he could read her mind, Papa said, "Lily, Mama and I thought it might be nice to attend the hymn singing tonight. It's always late by the time it's over, so if everyone takes a nap now, we can stay up a little longer tonight."

Well, that put the horrible afternoon-nap idea in an entirely different light. Lily was thrilled to hear they would be going to the hymn singing tonight. Her family didn't attend them very often. The singings were usually for the boys and girls who were old enough to start socializing. Lily could not *wait* until she turned sixteen and joined them. Oh, what a happy birthday that would be!

Lily ran to her room, changed her clothes, and jumped on the bed. She closed her eyes and tried to sleep but her mind was too busy making plans. She would sit beside Cousin Hannah and eavesdrop on the big girls' conversations. They tried to listen in to the eighth graders at school but were always shooed away. Whatever did those big girls have to talk about? They put their heads together and twittered like chickens.

She tried to imagine herself as a sixteen-year-old at a singing, sitting at a table with the rest of the big girls. In a flash, she realized that those big girls would be her friends. Would Hannah still be taller than her? Would Effie still have a puckered-up look on her face, like she'd just eaten a green persimmon? Lily grinned at the thought.

The next thing she knew, Mama was gently shaking her shoulder. "It's time to get ready for the singing."

Lily's eyes went wide. Had she really slept? She jumped out of bed and changed back into her Sunday clothes. She galloped downstairs to eat sandwiches Mama had prepared for a quick supper. The good thing about sandwiches was they didn't make a lot of dirty dishes. It didn't take long to get everything cleaned up, and then it was time to go to the singing. How fun! Lily skipped down the driveway, ahead of Mama and Papa and the boys.

Hannah was waiting at the end of her driveway for Lily to arrive. The girls ran to the front porch swing. They wanted to be able to watch all the buggies come in the driveway and stop in front of the house. The girls would get off the buggies and walk into the house while the boys went to unhitch the horses. Then the boys would stand around in a big group talking and laughing and horsing around until it was time to start singing.

Watching them, Lily thought it might be fun to be a boy. They were able to talk and laugh as loud as they pleased. Inside the house, the girls would stand in a clump and quietly visit. Only soft, gentle laughter allowed. In just about every way, boys had more fun than girls.

After they got bored watching the boys, Hannah suggested they go inside. Lily slid off the swing and followed Hannah into the house. The girls sat quietly at the table. Teacher Rhoda smiled at Lily and Hannah when she saw them and started paging through her little black hymnbook.

Lily hoped Teacher Rhoda would lead a few songs tonight. She had a beautiful voice. She wanted Papa and Mama to hear how lovely her voice was.

Soon, a noisy clomping sound hit the porch. It was the boys, coming in for the singing time. Hannah and Lily darted behind their parents and found a chair to sit on. They watched as the boys filed in and sat across the table from the girls.

Aaron Yoder's oldest brother, Samuel, the one who seemed all grown-up, announced the first song and everyone started to sing. It was pure heaven to Lily. She loved the sounds of harmony. In church, they sang in only one voice, no harmony. No one should stand out but they should all sing as one. But at singings, they could sing different parts. She knew every song and was able to keep up.

She watched as the girls shared two glasses that they filled with water from the pitcher that stood in the middle of the table. On the other side, the boys also had two glasses that they shared. Lily thought that was disgusting. She would never take a drink of water at a singing table once she was old enough to be part of the young folks.

A little later they passed a saltshaker around the table and anyone who was beginning to get hoarse from singing so long sprinkled a little into the palm of their hand and then licked it. Lily and Hannah both thought that was weird. They looked at each other and giggled. It was funny to see big boys and girls licking salt like a cow at a salt lick. Even Teacher Rhoda took a little salt.

After two hours of singing, one of the boys announced the closing hymn. It was one of Lily's favorite songs. It always made her feel happy and bouncy. She was sorry when it was over. The boys got up from the table and filed outside. The girls remained sitting at the table for a while longer visiting with each other. Quietly visiting, of course.

"Let's go outside and watch everyone leave," Hannah said.

Lily thought she should ask Mama, but she was busy talking to Aunt Mary. Baby Paul was sleeping in her lap.

So Lily quietly followed Hannah outside. They could hear the boys talking and laughing again. She wanted to sneak closer to them to hear what they were talking about. It sounded interesting.

"Let's hide here under this pine tree," Hannah said. "We can peek through the branches and watch to see who gets in the buggies."

It wasn't long before the first buggy drove up. In it was Carrie Kauffman's brother. He stopped at the house and Carrie walked down the porch steps and got on the buggy. As the buggy drove out the driveway, another buggy drove in. In this one was Samuel Yoder. Lily thought it was strange that he bothered to stop at the house. After all, he didn't have a sister. She was surprised to see Teacher Rhoda come out and get on the buggy and then they drove away together.

"Teacher Rhoda has a beau!" Hannah whispered. "She'll probably get married soon."

Wait. *What?* That was terrible news! She wanted Teacher Rhoda to always be her teacher and not ever get married. Especially not to a brother of Aaron Yoder.

Lily and Hannah went back inside. Papa and Mama were getting the little boys ready to go home. On the walk home, Lily asked Mama why Teacher Rhoda would take a ride with Aaron's brother.

Mama was not happy to hear that Lily and Hannah had been spying. "Teacher Rhoda and Aaron's brother are courting," she said.

"Will they get married?" Lily asked. *Please please please please please say no.*

"We'll have to wait and see," Mama said, but she had a twinkle in her eye. "I don't want you to say anything about it at school. The other children probably don't know and they don't need to find out through you. Understand?"

"Yes, Mama," Lily said. It would be fun to keep such an important secret. At least she finally knew something that

Effie Kauffman didn't know. "But if Teacher Rhoda marries Samuel, then she won't be my teacher anymore."

"Only time will tell," Mama said.

But what if time told Lily something she didn't want to hear?

The next evening, the boys went to sleep early and Lily was allowed to stay up. It was quiet in the living room. The only sounds were the clicking of Mama's knitting needles and the rustle of Papa's newspaper. Lily got tired of worrying quietly.

"It would be terrible if she stopped teaching!" Lily said very loudly, making Papa jump.

"Are you still worrying about Teacher Rhoda?" Mama said.

"Yes!" Lily said. "She will marry Samuel Yoder and never teach again!"

"Lily, you might be putting the cart before the horse," Papa said. "Even if that were to happen, then the school board would find another teacher for the school."

"What if we end up with another teacher like Teacher Katie?" Lily said. "It will be awful! Everyone will move away. We will move away. And then we will have to start all over again!"

"That's borrowing an awful lot of trouble," Papa said. He went back behind his newspaper.

Lily looked to Mama. "I don't know why anyone would want to get married and stop teaching school." Especially to someone related to Aaron Yoder.

"When you fall in love with someone, you're willing to give up some things," Mama said. "You'll see."

"Not me," Lily said. She couldn't think of one boy to love and marry. "I don't think I'll get married. I'm going to live with you and Papa for the rest of my life."

206

Papa dropped his paper and exchanged a smile with Mama. "You may feel different later on."

"I did," Mama said. "Love has a way of sneaking up on you when you least expect it."

Lily made a face. That sounded creepy.

"Like moonlight," Mama said. "It sneaks up on you like moonlight."

That sounded a little better.

"But how did you know it was love?"

Mama cast a sideways glance at Papa. "Whenever I was around Papa, I felt like I had butterflies in my tummy."

"Like you were sick?" Lily said, which made Papa laugh.

"No," Mama said. "They were romantic butterflies." Lily moved over to the couch and stared at Papa over the newspaper. He did not look romantic to her. He looked embarrassed. But pleased, too. More pleased than embarrassed.

"Did you ever hear how we met?" Mama said with a smile.

"Rachel," Papa said, grinning. His cheeks turned red.

"How?" Lily said. "What did Papa do?"

"It was at Sunday church, after lunch. I had helped wash dishes and went out on the porch to toss out the dirty wash water over the railing. But . . . I didn't look first. I threw the dishwater right at Papa's face!" She cringed at the memory, but it was a happy cringe.

"You did that?" Lily said. "Poor Papa!"

"I was just minding my own business, walking past the porch, whistling a happy tune, and suddenly a beautiful girl was tossing dirty dishwater at me." Papa laughed. "But after I got over the shock, I realized that beautiful girl had captured my heart." He winked at Mama. "It was love at first splash."

Mama's Birthday Cake

*M*ama's birthday was coming and Lily wanted to make her something special this year. She couldn't decide what to do. She dug through the basket of fabric scraps hoping for inspiration.

She had already tried making a pot holder for Mama. It hadn't turned out very well. Besides, Mama had plenty of good pot holders and didn't need more.

Lily put the fabric basket away again. She'd have to give this more thought. Maybe tomorrow. For now, Mama was calling to Lily from the kitchen to help her clean out the cupboards.

Mama had pulled out all of the cookbooks and stacked them on the floor. "Put the ones we don't use often in a different pile," she told her. So Lily sorted through the cookbooks and found one she hadn't seen. It had a glossy cover with a picture of a layer cake on the cover. "Cakes for All Occasions," it said in big red letters. Lily leafed through it, fascinated by the pictures of beautiful cakes.

She was suddenly hit with inspiration! She was going to make a beautiful birthday cake for Mama. She finished sorting the rest of the cookbooks and put them back into the cupboard. When Mama had gone upstairs to check on baby Paul, Lily grabbed the cake cookbook and ran with it to her bedroom. She tucked it in her top desk drawer. Tonight she would look through it and choose the cake she wanted to bake.

That evening, Lily lit her oil lamp and changed into her nightgown. She pulled out the cake cookbook. She wasn't at all hungry after a big dinner, but still, her mouth watered from the pictures. She paged through it slowly, looking carefully at every cake. Most of them seemed too hard to make or needed ingredients that she knew Mama didn't have in the pantry.

And then she found it: A beautiful marble cake with two layers and covered with lots of swirled fluffy frosting. She read the recipe several times to make sure she would have everything she needed and would know how to make it. It didn't sound very hard. *This* was the cake she was going to make. She rummaged through her desk and found a bookmark to save the place in the cookbook. Now she would have to figure out some way to make the cake without Mama finding out. She blew out the light and hopped into bed. She felt happy as she snuggled under the covers. Mama would be so pleased with the beautiful cake Lily was going to make for her.

During supper the next day, Mama took a bite of brownie and yelped. "Ouch!" She held her cheek with her hand.

"What's wrong, Rachel?" Papa asked.

"It's that tooth that's been bothering me," Mama said. "But it's much worse today. I should have known better than trying to eat a brownie with nuts."

"I'm going to make an appointment with a dentist for you before I start work in the shop this afternoon," Papa said. "I don't want you having to suffer from a painful tooth."

Lily felt sorry that Mama had to go to the dentist. Nobody wanted to go to the dentist. But then she realized this was the opportunity she'd been looking for! She could bake Mama's birthday cake while she was at the dentist.

Papa came back from the phone shanty. "You have an appointment for tomorrow afternoon at four o'clock," he said. "Mr. Tanner will be here to pick you up after three thirty."

The next day, Lily hurried home from school, hoping Mr. Tanner wouldn't be late. She kept glancing out the window to see if she could spot Mr. Tanner's car coming down the road. By the time he arrived, Mama looked around the kitchen. "Lily, put the casserole in the oven at five thirty. I'm going to drop the boys at Grandma Miller's until I get back."

That was wonderful news! Lily wasn't sure how she would get the cake baked if she had to watch Dannie and Paul. She waited until she saw Mr. Tanner's car turn onto the road, then ran upstairs to get the cookbook.

She read the instructions for the cake recipe: Preheat the oven to 350 degrees. Lily opened the door at the bottom of the kerosene stove and pulled the tray with the burners out to light them. She tipped the chimneys back and turned the wicks up. She took a match, struck it, and held the flame against the wick. As it traveled slowly around the wick she tried to lower the chimney gently. It got stuck and Lily jiggled it like she saw Mama do often. All of a sudden it went down fast and snuffed the flames. Lily tried again. The same thing happened. After several more tries she gave up and ran down the basement stairs and into the shop.

Papa was working at the drill press, drilling holes in the back of a chair seat. Lily explained that she was trying to bake a birthday cake for Mama and that she couldn't light the burners for the kerosene stove. Could he please help?

Papa went upstairs and lit the burners. Lily adjusted the flames until they were burning a nice blue flame. Now she could finally make the cake. She showed the picture of the cake she wanted to bake to Papa. "It looks good," he said, patting Lily's shoulder. "If you need any more help, just let me know."

Papa went back to his shop as Lily gathered the ingredients. She measured flour and sugar into the mixing bowl. She glanced at the clock and was bothered to see how much time she had wasted in trying to light the burners. She was afraid she wouldn't have enough time before Mama came home.

She finished stirring the batter. It was time to add the chocolate swirl into the batter to make it seem like a marble. She read the instructions and decided it would take too long to melt all the chocolate. She decided to pour the chocolate chips into the batter without melting them first. They could melt while they were baking. She thought this might be a brilliant idea. Every chocolate chip would melt into its own pretty little swirl. The cake would be filled with dainty swirls. It would be even prettier than the one in the cookbook.

Lily could just see Mama cutting the cake, oohing and aahing at how pretty the swirls were and asking Lily how she did it. She was sure Mama would be pleased with her swirl invention. For good measure, Lily added an extra cup full of chocolate chips to the cake batter and mixed it well.

She slid the cake pan into the stove and set the timer to make sure she would remember to take the cake out of the oven in time. It would never do to burn Mama's special chocolate swirl birthday cake.

Hurry, hurry, hurry! Lily glanced at the clock. She quickly washed the baking dishes while the cake was in the oven. She didn't want to leave a trace of her surprise. Then she paged through the cookbook again. In the back she found all kinds of frosting recipes. Lily read the different recipes and one caught her eye: Lemon Icing. Lily read through the instructions and thought it sounded even easier than plain old butter cream frosting. She measured powdered sugar into a bowl, added lemon juice and stirred. Instead of getting fluffy like frosting was supposed to, it looked thin and watery. She was trying to figure out how to fix it when the timer rang.

Lily quickly removed the cake from the oven and put it into the refrigerator to cool before Mama came home. She read through the icing recipe again to see what she had done wrong but she had done exactly what the recipe had told her to do. She sprinkled more powdered sugar into the bowl and stirred. The frosting was still too thin.

So Lily decided to add food coloring. If the frosting wasn't going to be fluffy, at least it could be pretty. She dug through the pantry until she found the box with the food coloring. On the back of the box she found instructions on how to make different colors. It looked easy! You just added different food colorings together. Lily decided on a beautiful purple frosting. It would be the prettiest frosting ever.

Lily measured in red food coloring to the lemon icing, then

added blue. Instead of turning purple, it turned into a sickly orange-brown color. Lily felt like crying. All her wonderful plans weren't working out the way she had hoped.

Then she heard the crunch of tires on the gravel in the driveway. Mama was home! She grabbed the cake from the refrigerator and the bowl of frosting and ran upstairs with them. She sat on the floor in her room and poured the frosting on top of the cake. She tried to spread it out nicely but it turned into an orange-brown puddle in the middle of the sunken cake. Finally, Lily gave up. She put the cake into her bottom desk drawer and hid the dirty mixing bowl in her closet.

"Lily," Mama called up the stairs. "Did you remember to put the casserole in the oven?"

Oops.

Supper would be very late tonight.

Three days later was Mama's birthday. At the supper table Papa gave Mama a big box. Lily watched eagerly as Mama opened it because Papa always gave good gifts. Mama drew out a pretty towel set. She stroked it happily. "Thank you, Daniel," she said. "It's just what we needed. It will look so pretty in the bathroom."

When it was time for dessert, Papa said, "I think Lily has something for Mama's birthday now."

Lily ran upstairs and got the cake out of her desk drawer. The sickly orange frosting looked even worse than it had when Lily had put it on the cake. She carried it downstairs and gave it to Mama. "Happy birthday, Mama," she said, a little uncertainly.

But Mama looked so pleased! She cut a piece for everyone. Joseph and Dannie, who normally ate everything, picked at it with odd expressions on their faces. Papa tried one bite and froze. "Lemon icing? On top of a chocolate chip cake?" he said, as if that might be a strange combination.

Lily was disappointed to discover the chocolate chips hadn't melted at all. They still looked like chocolate chips instead of pretty little swirls. And because she had added so many in the batter, the cake was crumbly.

Mama didn't seem to notice all the mistakes, not even the disgusting color of the icing. "It's so nice to have a daughter big enough to bake a cake by herself," she said. She finished her piece of cake and then said, "I think I need a second helping," and cut another piece.

Mama never had second helpings of dessert. Not ever. She must have really loved that cake recipe. Lily thought she might make it for her every year.

Teacher Rhoda's Horrible News

oday was the last day of school. Teacher Rhoda stood by her desk, giving her end-of-the-term speech. This time, she added a shocker: "I have enjoyed all the years I spent being your teacher, but when school starts again in the fall you will be getting a new teacher."

The classroom went bone silent. Then someone—maybe Lily—began to cry, and soon all of the girls were sniffing loudly and quietly crying.

"Why aren't you coming back in the fall?" Effie asked.

Effie always asked the questions everyone was thinking. Usually, it was annoying. Not today, though. Lily was glad to hear Effie pipe up.

An embarrassed little smile spread across Teacher Rhoda's face. "I'll be very busy with some other plans. But I'm sure you will learn to like your new teacher and enjoy school just as much as you do now."

Lily and Cousin Hannah exchanged a knowing look. She had been afraid of this moment—ever since that first Sunday evening singing when she and Hannah had spied on the youth at Uncle Elmer's house and saw Teacher Rhoda get into Samuel Yoder's buggy.

The tears were coming faster now, too fast for Lily to wipe away. Teacher Rhoda might not be telling them but she was sure those other plans included marrying Aaron Yoder's older brother. How sad!

In the kitchen, Lily was helping Mama fold sun-dried laundry from the clothesline. "Mama, how old were you when you decided you wanted to court Papa?"

Mama tucked a sheet under her chin and folded up the sides. "Around Teacher Rhoda's age, I suppose."

Lily's head swam. "How did you know you wanted to court Papa?"

"Well, you know about how I threw the dishwater at Papa."

Lily grinned. "I remember."

Mama plucked a towel, stiff from the sun, out of the laundry basket and folded it in half. "But we didn't talk that night, other than when I apologized to him for dousing him with dirty dishwater." She smiled. "I had cousins who lived in Papa's community, so I knew a little bit about him. Papa was awfully shy. We saw each other now and then, but he never spoke to me."

"Never?"

"Not until a certain weekend. My cousins were having church

at their house. It was an in-between Sunday for our church, so my friends and I decided to walk over to my cousins' and stay the night. We would be able to go to church the next day."

"And you could see Papa."

Mama smiled. "Then I could see Papa."

"So what happened?"

Mama put down the socks she had been folding. "We left in the morning, right after breakfast, bright as buttons. Very cheerful and excited. We started walking. And walking. And walking. My sister, your aunt Mary, got a blister on her heel. I slowed down to stay with her and soon we had fallen way behind the other girls. What we hadn't realized was how far fifteen miles of walking could actually be!"

"Did you turn around?"

"We discussed it. By now, we couldn't even see my friends. They were that far ahead of us. I wasn't even sure we were heading in the right direction anymore. But next thing we knew, a horse and buggy pulled up beside us."

"Papa?"

"Yes, it was Papa. He offered us a ride. He drove us right to my cousins' house and took us all the way home again the next day. It was the first time we talked to each other."

"And we haven't stopped talking yet," Papa said as he walked into the kitchen. He had been listening the whole time. He gave Mama his special smile that made Lily feel as if they had forgotten she was in the room. Mama returned the smile.

"I think we'll have to pick strawberries tomorrow," Mama said. "I want you to take a note to Aunt Mary. She said she would help us pick them when they're ripe."

Lily had been eyeing the strawberry patch for days, watching the berries get plump and red. She loved to eat strawberries and she didn't even mind picking a few. But Mama and Papa had planted an entire acre with thousands of strawberry plants. The very sight of that strawberry field exhausted her! But having her relatives come to help would make it fun.

Lily ran all the way to Aunt Mary's house and found her in the garden, pulling weeds with Hannah. Aunt Mary read the note Lily handed to her. She smiled at Lily. "Tell your mother that I'll come over tomorrow to help pick strawberries."

On the way home, Lily was struck with a brilliant idea. Even with Aunt Mary's help, it would take days, weeks maybe, to get all those strawberries picked. She was sure Grandpa and Grandma Miller would come help if they knew that Mama needed them. She was almost walking by Grandma's mailbox, and before she could think twice, she turned into their driveway, walked up to the porch, and knocked on the door.

Grandma opened the door and looked surprised to see Lily.

"We need help picking strawberries tomorrow," Lily said.

"Aunt Susie and I will be there bright and early tomorrow morning," Grandma said.

Lily was pleased. On the way back to the house, she decided not to tell Mama. Grandma's appearance tomorrow would be a nice surprise for her.

❧✦❧

The sun was peeping in the eastern horizon the next morning when Aunt Mary arrived. Lily was still clearing breakfast dishes away. Aunt Mary had brought along Levi, Hannah, and Davy.

"The dishes can wait today," Mama told her. She handed

out baskets and everyone headed out to the strawberry patch.
By the time Grandma and Aunt Susie arrived, Lily had filled
her basket.

Mama was surprised to see Grandma. Even more surprised when she heard that Lily had asked them to come.
She raised her eyebrows at Lily, as if to say, "We'll talk later
about asking others for help without permission." She turned
to Grandma and told her that she would help her get started
sorting and selling the berries in the little roadside stand that
Papa had built.

219

Grandma sat behind the counter sorting strawberries. Only the biggest, juiciest, nicest ones were put into little baskets to be sold. Mama gave Grandma a bowl for the smaller berries. They would be used to make jam and pie filling. In between customers, Grandma could sort berries.

It took only two days for Lily to be sick and tired of strawberries. Even thinking about Mama's strawberry shortcake or strawberry jam didn't help. New strawberries kept ripening and the work was endless, even with Aunt Mary, Hannah, and Levi's help. As soon as they had finished picking the last row, it was time to start on the first row again.

Mama and Aunt Mary liked to sing while they worked. The first few days, Lily and Hannah had sung along. Singing wasn't fun any longer. The only interesting part of picking strawberries was eavesdropping on Mama and Aunt Mary's conversations, in between songs.

Hannah was just as weary of picking strawberries as Lily. The girls picked slower and slower. To help pass the time, they made plans for things to do after strawberry season was over.

"I'm going to take long walks in the woods," Hannah said. "Maybe I'll walk past Aaron Yoder's house."

Lily ignored that. She wanted to sit and read one of her books for a whole day without having to do anything else.

Mama and Aunt Mary had stopped singing and were talking. Lily sidled closer to the row they were working on. Eavesdropping on them was better than nothing.

"How is the mini barn business?" Mama said.

"It's doing well," Aunt Mary said. "Elmer has built the barns in between his fieldwork. He's been busy. But we've already sold a few." She stood and put her hands on her hips, stretching her back. "That reminds me! Last evening,

Elmer and I thought it might be a nice treat for the children to camp overnight in a mini barn after strawberry season is over. They've all been working so hard."

"That sounds like a fun idea," Mama said. "I'll talk it over with Daniel, but I don't see why they couldn't enjoy a little campout."

Lily and Hannah looked at each other, mouths open to a big O. A campout sounded like fun! They both began picking strawberries faster and faster. The sooner the last strawberry was picked, the sooner they could have their overnight.

CHAPTER

35

Late Night Visiting

Strawberry season finally came to an end. On a beautiful, warm Sunday evening, Lily and Joseph were packing up to spend a night camping with their cousins. Dannie was in a bad mood because he was told he was too young to join them, but other than that, it was an exciting event.

Papa and Mama sat on the front porch swing. Papa held Paul in his lap and Dannie sat between Mama and Papa, sad and sorry for himself. Lily and Joseph waved goodbye and started down the road. They carried their overnight things in shopping bags. Lily had packed her prettiest nightgown. Joseph had stuffed into his bag the first pair of pajamas he could find in his room.

Cousins Levi and Hannah were waiting outside for them, eager to get the campout under way. They had already spread blankets and pillows in two mini barns. Aunt Mary had popped popcorn. The children sat on the front porch, eating popcorn, talking, and laughing, until it was time for bed.

Levi, Davy, and Joseph went into the boys' mini barn and Lily and Hannah went into the other one. The girls took turns changing into their nightgowns. Lily stood outside the mini barn while she waited for Hannah to change. She noticed a lot of fireflies fluttering around. Their little lights blinked on and off. It would be fun to try to catch some before they settled down to sleep. "Hurry, Hannah!"

Hannah opened the door. "All ready," she said.

"Let's catch some fireflies!" Lily said.

"That would be fun," Hannah said. She and Lily ran to the basement to get jars to hold the fireflies they caught. As they came out of the basement, they saw three white ghosts tiptoe toward the girls' mini barn.

Lily and Hannah stopped abruptly, hearts pounding.

"The boys are hiding under sheets," Hannah whispered. "They think we're inside the mini barn. They think they're scaring us."

They waited to see what the boys were going to do next. They had to cover their mouths to keep from laughing out loud when they saw them pick up sticks and scratch the side of the mini barn, making funny groaning noises.

"Let's fill up plastic bottles with water," Hannah said. "We can sneak up behind them and squirt them."

They tiptoed back to the basement, careful not to slam the door or make any noise to alert the boys that they weren't inside their mini barn.

They filled two bottles with water. Carefully, they sneaked up behind the boys and squeezed the bottles as hard as they could. The boys yelled and screamed, running back to their mini barn. Lily and Hannah chased behind, laughing and squirting water.

The noise brought Uncle Elmer outside to see what the ruckus was all about. His gaze took in the soaked sheets on the ground, then shifted to the empty bottles in the girls' hands. He listened, eyes twinkling, to Hannah's explanation. "Okay, I think there has been enough excitement for one evening," he said. "Time to get some sleep. Hannah, you go inside and bring some dry sheets out for the boys. Then it's time to get to bed. No more visiting each other's mini barns. Understand?"

"Yes," chimed five voices.

Lily went back to the girls' mini barn and sat on her blanket, waiting for Hannah to come back. Hannah returned and sat next to her. They both laughed at turning the tables on the boys. It was so easy! They were too wide awake from excitement to go to sleep.

"Do you think Samuel Yoder took Teacher Rhoda home from the singing again tonight?" Hannah asked.

"Probably," Lily said. "Mama says that they're courting."

"I hope they don't get married until we turn sixteen," Hannah said. "I think weddings will be more fun after we're old enough to be a part of the youth group."

"I just hope she waits to get married until we graduate so we can help with the wedding. Just four more years." Lily stretched out on the blanket and leaned on her elbows. "I wonder what they do."

"Who? What?" Hannah asked.

"Samuel and Rhoda," Lily said. "I wonder what they do for courting."

The girls lay quietly for a moment, chins on their palms,

pondering the mysteries of courting. Hannah's face lit up. "Why don't we go see? Teacher Rhoda's home isn't very far away. Only through the woods and over a few fields. We could run over and peep through their windows."

"But it's dark outside," Lily said. "And your father said we need to stay in our mini barns."

"No, he didn't," Hannah said. "He said we couldn't go visiting in each other's mini barns. We won't be doing *that*." Which was an example of how Hannah reasoned. "I have a flashlight and the moon is shining brightly." She jumped to her feet. "Come on. Let's go!"

"In our nightgowns?" Lily asked.

"Of course!" Hannah said. "No one will see us."

Lily held her breath as Hannah opened the door. The hinges creaked noisily, echoing in the still of the night. She was sure that Uncle Elmer could hear it and would come see what they were doing.

It was a warm night. There were no other sounds besides chirping crickets, singing katydids, and the distant sound of a few night birds trilling in the woods. Lily and Hannah hurried out the driveway and across the road. Along the way, they discussed what they were going to do, knowing it was wrong but lured by its daring.

Then they came to the woods. The trees rose like towering giants. The moonlight sifted through the branches and cast flickering shadows on the floor of the woods. Every step they took seemed to make noise. Twigs snapped, leaves crunched. The woods seemed alive with spooky noises. Lily's heart beat fast as she tried to stay close to Hannah. She wanted to go right back to the mini barn and call it a night. Hannah wasn't scared at all. She just kept on marching through the woods in her nightgown, shining the flashlight on the path ahead of them.

Lily was relieved to come out on the other side of the woods. Now there were only two cornfields and a hayfield to cross before they reached Teacher Rhoda's home. The cornstalks weren't even up to their knees yet, so walking through the field was easy. They followed the rows and stepped over plants.

Unfortunately, the plan started to unravel as soon as they entered Teacher Rhoda's yard. A dog started to bark. Loud and scary. Lily and Hannah stopped in their tracks. The dog ran around the corner of the house, barking at them. But when he saw them, he wagged his tail and came over to be petted. Lily stroked his head and whispered, "Please don't bark anymore." The dog wiggled all over as if he understood what Lily had said.

Hannah pointed to a window. "I think they must be in there. Do you see the lamplight?"

Holding hands, the girls tiptoed up the porch steps. They froze when a wooden board creaked underneath their feet. They crossed the porch to peek into the living room window. The dog followed behind them and sat down, his tail beating a steady *thump*, *thump*, *thump* against the floor. Lily and Hannah peered inside. Samuel and Rhoda were sitting on a sofa, eating popcorn from a bowl and talking.

What a disappointment! Had they walked all this way in the middle of the night just to see them talk?

Hannah was disappointed, too. "Let's go," she whispered. They turned around and started down the porch steps. The dog walked beside them, his toenails clicking against the wood. Hannah walked down a few steps and then jumped to the bottom. The dog crossed in front of her to dart after Hannah, causing Lily to trip. She tumbled down to the bottom of the stairs.

Lily jumped up, smoothing her nightgown. Suddenly, the door opened and there stood Samuel and Teacher Rhoda.

"What are you girls doing here?" Teacher Rhoda asked.

Lily and Hannah looked at each other. How awful to have been caught spying on them! "We wanted to see what people do when they are courting," Hannah said.

Samuel and Teacher Rhoda stood looking at them. Lily wished she could disappear. She felt so foolish—standing at the foot of the porch steps in her nightgown. The silly dog sat beside her like they were best friends.

Lily managed to look disinterested. "Well, we'll just be on our way. We won't bother you again."

"It's about time I head for home," Samuel said. "I can give you a ride."

"We can walk," Lily and Hannah said at the same time. What if he were to tell Uncle Elmer? Oh, this was terrible.

"Nonsense," Samuel said. "Let me go get my horse and we'll be on our way." He didn't sound mad. He sounded amused.

Quiet followed as Lily and Hannah climbed on Samuel's buggy and sat there like stones. Miserable stones. This fun spying adventure had turned out to be a disaster. What would their parents say when they found out what they had done?

Samuel's horse trotted briskly down the road. Lily was torn between wanting this ride to be over and not wanting to get home. "Lily is spending the night at our house," Hannah said.

"It's always nice when cousins can have fun together," Samuel said. But instead of taking both of them to Uncle Elmer's house, Samuel turned into Lily's driveway. He jumped off the buggy and tied his horse to the hitching post. He waved to Lily to climb down. Then he walked up to the front porch with her.

Lily wanted to run and hide when Samuel knocked on the door. She heard Papa's footsteps and then the door opened. He looked back and forth between Samuel and Lily.

"Lily and Hannah thought it would be fun to spy on a courting couple," Samuel said.

Papa looked at her. "Ah. I see. I'm sorry, Samuel. Lily, go inside."

Lily ran up the stairs to her room and jumped into bed. She could hear Papa and Samuel talk for a little and then the crunch of buggy wheels on the gravel driveway as Samuel took Hannah home.

Papa and Mama came into Lily's bedroom. They stood looking at her. Lily felt as if she had never been looked at so much in her life as she had this evening. She wanted to pull the covers up over her head. She didn't, but she wanted to.

"I'm sorry to hear what you and Hannah did tonight," Mama said.

"Little girls have no business wandering the countryside at night and peering into other people's homes," Papa said. "No more sleepovers until we're sure we can trust you to behave. I want you to promise us that you will never go spying on anyone ever again. Not ever."

"I promise," Lily whispered. *That*, she thought, wouldn't be hard to remember.

Uncle Jacob preached the main sermon at church that week, his first. He did a fine job of preaching. He was Lily's favorite minister, and not just because he was her uncle. His preaching was so easy to listen to that even she could understand what he was talking about.

Everyone sat down after the benediction. Lily reached for the hymnbook, tucked under the bench, expecting to hear him announce where church would be held next.

But no! Uncle Jacob rose to his feet for a special announcement. "Two young people, with the blessings of their parents, want to get married. They are Samuel Yoder and Rhoda King. The wedding will be a week from Thursday."

Hannah nudged Lily with her elbow. "Told you," she whispered. Then Uncle Jacob sat down and the song leader announced the last song. Everyone started to sing as if nothing unusual had just happened. Lily tried to see if Teacher Rhoda's face was turning red. Lily would feel mortified if she heard her name announced in church for everyone to hear. It was another very good reason to not get married.

As soon as the song ended, Samuel and Teacher Rhoda rose and walked outside. By the time church was dismissed, they had driven off in Samuel's buggy.

How mysterious! Lily wondered what could be so important that they were missing out on church lunch and an afternoon of visiting with their friends. She searched out Mama to ask, "Where did Teacher Rhoda and Samuel go?"

Mama smiled. "They went to write wedding invitations."

That would mean they had to write hundreds of invitations. Weddings were huge events—everyone was invited. Lily's hands felt achy just thinking about writing so many invitations.

Another excellent reason to never get married.

Teacher Rhoda's Wedding

It was a beautiful summer morning in June. The sky was bright blue and the air had a touch of sweet summer breeze. Not too cold, not too hot. Just right. As soon as breakfast was over, Lily dressed in her dark blue Sunday dress. She still needed help pinning her cape and apron so she ran downstairs to find Mama. Everything had to be perfect, even Lily's pins. Today was Teacher Rhoda's wedding day!

Mama was dressed in her dark blue Sunday dress, too. All the women and girls would wear blue dresses.

It still troubled Lily to think Teacher Rhoda was going to marry a brother of Aaron Yoder. She hoped Teacher Rhoda wouldn't regret that decision. Had she really thought this through? Lily thought not. After all, every family gathering would mean that Teacher Rhoda would have to see Aaron. She could never, ever avoid him. Lily shivered. How dreadful!

From every direction, horses and buggies were streaming

toward the farm where Teacher Rhoda would be married. So many people came from neighboring church districts. Buggy horses walked up every hill and Jim had to slow down and try to walk patiently behind them.

When they reached the farm, Lily felt alarmed. There were so many people! Too many. She would get swallowed up in this sea of people. If she were nine, she would be expected to stay by Mama's side. Now that she was ten, she could be with her friends. But she couldn't find any friends.

Then she spotted Effie Kauffman. Even Effie's face was a welcome sight today. She hurried through the crowd to join Effie; soon Beth, Malinda, and Cousin Hannah found them, but no one had anything to say to each other. They felt shy and awkward, waiting until it was time to go out to the barn. Teacher Rhoda's family had set benches in the neatly swept haymow for all the wedding guests.

When the service began, Lily soon grew bored. Weddings were just like church. The preachers kept talking and talking and talking. Didn't they ever run out of words? She wished they would hurry along and get to the main event: the wedding ceremony of Teacher Rhoda and Samuel Yoder.

Lily glanced up at the clock that someone had hung on one of the rafters at the far side of the barn. It was almost noon. No wonder she was hungry. Bishop Henry started to slow down his windy preaching. That was a good sign. Lily wanted to clap when she heard him say, "Samuel and Rhoda, if you are still willing to be married, you can come stand in front of me."

Lily watched as Samuel and Teacher Rhoda walked up and stood next to each other in front of Bishop Henry. Their backs were turned to the rest of the room. Teacher Rhoda looked pretty in her blue dress and crisply starched white cape and apron. She seemed tiny compared to Samuel.

Bishop Henry asked Samuel and Teacher Rhoda some questions. They answered so softly that Lily almost couldn't hear them. Next, the bishop asked everyone to stand while he read a prayer. At the end of the prayer, everyone sat down. Bishop Henry reached for Samuel and Teacher Rhoda's hands and clasped them together. He prayed for a blessing on their married life. And then Samuel and Teacher Rhoda went back to their seats.

Lily felt let down. All of this excitement . . . for *that*? Getting married didn't look like much fun.

As everyone sang the final song, Teacher Rhoda's father signaled to a few men. They left the barn to hitch horses to several buggies. It was time for the cooks and table waiters to get the meal ready for the guests.

Everyone waited patiently until the bridal party drove away. Then, the barn came alive! Jostling and bumping occurred as everyone tried to leave at the same time. Women and children went to the house to get their bonnets. They visited with each other in small clumps in the yard while they waited for buggies to drive up to the house. Lily was glad to see Papa heading toward them in the buggy. Lily and Mama climbed in the buggy and followed other buggies down the road to Teacher Rhoda's home.

Mama handed a wedding gift to Lily for her to carry while Mama followed with Paul. Lily felt important as she carried the gift into the house. Papa had made a beautiful magazine rack and Mama had wrapped it in several towels. Lily was sure Teacher Rhoda and Samuel would like their gift best of all.

"Lily, you can take the gift upstairs," Mama said. "Place

it on the bed with the rest of the gifts." Lily walked up the stairs. She wasn't sure which bedroom had all the gifts. She tiptoed down the hallway and peeked in a room where she heard voices. There were Samuel and Teacher Rhoda! They were sitting on the floor, opening gifts. The bed was buried under a mountain of gifts. Teacher Rhoda smiled when she saw Lily at the door. "Come in!"

Lily handed her gift to Teacher Rhoda, feeling shy. She couldn't look at Samuel. Then she wondered what she should do next. She would have liked to have seen what all the gifts were but none of the other little girls were in that room, so she thought she should leave. Seeing all those gifts made her think twice about getting married. It was the first sign that getting married might be fun. Someday.

Lily turned around to leave Teacher Rhoda and Samuel to their gifts. She saw Hannah wave to her down the hallway. In another bedroom, the girls had gathered to sit and chat until it was time to eat. Teacher Rhoda's father was the one who called up the stairs, announcing it was time to eat. He directed each person so he or she would know where to sit. There was a certain way to do everything in Lily's church, especially weddings.

The little girls were seated last, so Lily spent time looking over all the tables. They were set with beautiful chinaware. Every family had loaned their best china for the wedding. She tried to see which table held Mama's china. Samuel and Teacher Rhoda had come to their house just this week to borrow it. Beth nudged her. She pointed to the table where the girls were supposed to sit. "That's our china," she whispered.

Lily admired the pattern. It all looked so beautiful.

After everyone had been seated, Bishop Henry spoke over

the noisy hum of visiting. "Now that everyone has gathered to eat, let's have a moment of silence as we thank the Lord."

The room grew quiet until Bishop Henry lifted his head and cleared his throat. Then the visiting began again—quietly at first, then louder and louder. From where Lily sat, she could watch the bridal party. Teacher Rhoda looked very happy as she sat next to Samuel.

Soon, the table waiters carried big platters and bowls to the table: golden fried chicken and bowls of steaming mashed potatoes, followed by sweet corn and a seven-layer salad. Everything looked so delicious! But Lily took only small portions. She was waiting for the best part. Dessert. Weddings always had plenty of desserts.

First, the table waiters brought out fruit and several cakes.

They looked good, but Lily ate fruit and cake at home. She passed on those. Next came pies. Every variety Lily could think of: cherry, apple, peach, blueberry, mixed fruit, lemon, vanilla, banana cream, pecan, shoo-fly, and several other kinds that she didn't even recognize. The only one she wanted was cherry pie. That was Grandpa Miller's favorite and that was her favorite.

But she was still waiting for something even better. Pudding! There were three kinds: tapioca, chocolate, and vanilla layered, and Lily's favorite: traditional Sweetheart Pudding. It was layered with sugared, toasted nuts and had a graham cracker–streusel topping. As she spooned it into her mouth, it tasted even better than it looked. Sweetheart Pudding was the second reason she might consider getting married someday. Gifts first—then pudding.

After everyone was done eating, the table waiters cleared off the dishes. They left the water glasses. Teacher Rhoda's father handed everyone a songbook. Visiting quieted as someone announced a song and everyone started singing. Lily liked singing. All afternoon they sat there and sang one song after another. Waiters kept fresh, cold water in everyone's glasses. Now and then, bowls of candy were passed around the tables. Lily always took a piece and put it in her pocket. Soon her pockets were filling up. She was still full from the delicious meal. The candy would taste even better if she saved it to eat later.

Too soon, the singing was over and it was time to go home. The wedding celebration would last until late at night, but Lily wouldn't be old enough to stay with the youth until she was sixteen.

After such a day, how could she sleep a wink?

Summer of Kangaroos

Lily looked up from the book she had been reading in the shade of the big maple tree. Joseph and Dannie stood in front of her, fishing poles in one hand and an old tin can filled with wiggling earthworms in the other. "Will you go fishing with us?" Joseph said. "We'll bait your hook if you come with us."

Fishing was the only thing Joseph and Dannie wanted to do, ever since Papa had taught them how to fish. Lily liked to sit beside the creek, but she didn't like fishing. She didn't like to touch slimy earthworms or scaly fish.

Dannie peered at her, an eager look on his round four-year-old face. "Mama said you can go with us if you want to."

Lily closed her book. "I'll go if you bait the hook *and* take care of any fish I happen to catch." She took her book inside and went down to the basement to get her fishing pole.

They walked down the driveway and across the road to reach a little path that skirted the edge of Papa's hayfield. The path veered off into the shady woods. During the long summer days, Lily liked to walk in the cool woods. Feathery ferns and wildflowers covered the ground. Splashes of sunlight filtered through the leafy branches of the towering trees. They tramped a mile, easy. Lily could smell the creek before they got near it. It had its own smell: sweet slow-moving water, fish, warm pine trees.

As soon as they reached the creek, they found their favorite spots to sit. Joseph baited Lily's hook first, and she tossed it into the water. She allowed it to drift for a little while, then slowly reeled it in and tossed it back into the water again. She hoped she wouldn't catch anything. Reeling and tossing were fun as long as she didn't catch a fish.

Dannie caught the first fish. Joseph helped him remove it and attach it to a line until they were ready to go back to the house.

Lily reeled her line in, then tossed it back out. It created a little splash in the water. She waited, then reeled it back in, but the hook had snagged on something. She jiggled the fishing pole, but the hook wouldn't come loose. "My line is stuck."

"I'll get it for you," Joseph said, reeling his line in. He placed the fishing pole on the ground, then cuffed his pant legs up above his knees before he waded into the creek.

Lily watched as he ran his hand along the line. Joseph took a few more steps and suddenly—*kersplash!*—he disappeared. His head popped up, but his neck was just barely above the water. "Stand up!" Lily yelled.

"I can't!" Joseph yelped. "I think my foot broke!" Lily tossed her fishing pole to the ground and waded into the water to see if she could help Joseph. She grabbed hold of Joseph's arm and started to pull. He made a horrible sound, like a cat having its tail stepped on. "Go get Papa!"

"I'll stay right here, Joseph," Dannie said. "Hurry, Lily!"

Lily waded to the edge of the creek and ran as fast as she could, the image of Joseph stuck in the creek firmly on her mind. What if the water started rising? What if a tidal wave came along? She had read about those in a book. He wasn't a very good swimmer. What if he drowned? Oh, that would be awful. She ran faster.

She stumbled through the tall grass, her skirt wet and heavy and clumsy as it slapped against her legs. Her breath came in gasps but still she ran on. She had to get to Mama and Papa and get help for Joseph.

It was hard to run up a hill. Lily's side pinched and she wanted to stop, to lay down and rest, to catch her breath. But fear of Joseph drowning in the creek kept her running. And what about Dannie? She could just imagine him drowning, too. He did everything Joseph did. Her legs felt numb and wooden as her feet kept pounding against the ground. She could see the house behind the cornstalks. Only a little farther now.

She burst into Papa's woodworking shop. He was putting a chair seat through the planer and couldn't hear her over the noise. Lily ducked through the spray of wood shavings to stand in front of him. Papa took one look at Lily's worried face and her dripping wet dress—now coated with shavings. He quickly pulled the lever to stop the hydraulic motor and the planer whined to a stop. "What's wrong?"

"Joseph is stuck in the creek," Lily said. "He thinks his foot is broken and I'm afraid he's drowning. Dannie, too."

Papa ran out of the shop and Lily trotted behind him as fast as she could, but her side still pinched. It took half the time, with Papa setting the pace. When they reached the creek, Lily was relieved to see that Joseph's head was still safely above the water. The tidal wave hadn't come.

Joseph and Dannie were both wailing at the top of their lungs. "Don't cry," Papa said. "Don't cry, boys. I'll get you out in a hurry." He removed his shoes, rolled up his pant legs, and waded into the creek. When he reached Joseph, he tried to lift him out of the water but stopped as Joseph let out a sharp cry.

"It's stuck!" Joseph said. "My foot is stuck on something."

Papa reached into the water and removed a rock that had trapped Joseph's foot. He gathered Joseph into his arms and waded back out of the creek. Gently, Papa set Joseph under a tree while he slipped back into his shoes. Then he picked him up again and carried him all the way back to the house. Lily held Dannie's hand and followed behind Papa. They had reached the house before Lily realized she had forgotten to bring the fishing poles. They were still on the creek bank. The hook of her pole was still snagged on something at the bottom of the creek. Probably that very same rock that had snagged Joseph.

Papa set Joseph on the kitchen table. Mama checked his foot.

"I think it's only a sprain," Mama said.

"It would be best to go have it x-rayed, just to make sure," Papa said. "I'll go call Mr. Tanner to come take us to the doctor."

Mama helped Joseph change into clean, dry clothes while Lily took Dannie and Paul out to the sandbox to play.

Soon, Mr. Tanner arrived in his big car. Lily pressed her nose against the kitchen window as she watched Papa and Joseph ride away with him.

"We left our fishing poles by the creek," Lily said to Mama. "Mine is stuck."

"Let's go get them," Mama said. "It'll get our minds off worrying about Joseph's foot."

Back to the creek for the third time today! Lily and Mama

took turns carrying Paul when he got tired of walking or running, which was often.

When they arrived, Mama tried to reel in the line on Lily's fishing pole, but she couldn't get it in, either. "I don't want to wade in the creek," Mama said. "We have plenty of fishing line and fish hooks back at the house. There's no need to have two family members spraining ankles in the creek today." She reached into her pocket and drew out small sewing scissors to snip the line. It always amazed Lily that Mama had just the right tools for the job in her pocket. Just in time!

Mama picked up the fish that Dannie had caught and handed it to him to carry back to the house. He held it up high, as if it were a giant shark rather than a tiny fish. Mama gathered up the rest of the fishing poles.

Later that afternoon, Lily heard a car pull into the driveway. She ran to the kitchen window and watched Papa get out of Mr. Tanner's car. He reached into the backseat and removed a small pair of crutches. Joseph scooted to the edge of the seat and then balanced himself on the crutches. He hopped to the house on the crutches, looking like a kangaroo. Crutches looked like fun to Lily.

"It's not broken," Papa said. "Joseph has a bad sprain. The doctor wants him to use crutches for a few weeks until his ankle feels better."

Lily was glad to hear that Joseph had not broken his ankle. She couldn't wait, though, to try out his crutches and hop around the house. Dannie was eyeing them, too, with the very same plan to borrow those crutches each time Joseph sat down. This, she decided right then and there, would be called the summer of kangaroos.

The Taffy Pull

On a Saturday morning in late July, Joseph ran into the house. "Lily! Look what the mailman brought for us!" He waved an envelope in her face.

Lily looked at the envelope. It was addressed to Lily and Joseph Lapp. "Give it to me," Lily said, reaching for it.

"It has my name on it too," Joseph said. He held it behind his back, keeping it away from her.

"My name is first," Lily said. She was the oldest. That role came with privileges.

Joseph's face fell. "But I hardly ever get mail. You get lots of letters."

That was true. She received a letter at least three times a year. "Well then, I'll let you open it, but I should be the one to read it first," Lily said. Since she was oldest, she needed to be the first informed for every event—big or small.

Joseph happily agreed. He was still young enough for Lily

to trick, but she knew it wouldn't last much longer. He opened the envelope and handed the letter inside to Lily.

Lily unfolded it and glanced at the signature. *Rhoda Yoder*. A letter from Teacher Rhoda! She cleared her throat the way Bishop Henry did before he was about to say something important. Then she began to read out loud.

Dear Lily and Joseph,
Next Saturday, I am hosting a taffy pull for all the children whom I used to teach. It will be at our new home at one o'clock in the afternoon.
I hope you both can come.

Sincerely,
Rhoda Yoder

"What's a taffy pull?" Joseph asked.

"I don't know," Lily said. "I've never been to a taffy pull."

Lily ran to find Mama and show her the letter. "Can we go?"

Mama read the letter. "That sounds like fun. We'll see what Papa has to say about it after lunch is ready."

Joseph, who usually disappeared when there was kitchen work to be done, helped Lily set the table. Like Lily, he wanted lunch to be ready as soon as possible. Mama was at the stove, boiling potatoes. She drained the liquid off the potatoes and reached for the potato masher. She looked up to find Lily and Joseph watching every move she made. She smiled. "You can go tell Papa lunch is ready. The potatoes will be ready by the time everyone is washed up."

Joseph ran to the shop. Lily listened for the band saw to shut down. She heard a hiss of air as Papa blew all the sawdust and shavings off his clothes with the air hose nozzle. She heard a bang: the door of the shop shut. Time for washing up. Lily quickly filled a pitcher with water to fill the glasses while Mama dished out mounds of fluffy mashed potatoes.

Papa barely eased into his chair before Lily popped the question. "Teacher Rhoda invited us to a taffy pull on Saturday. Can we go?"

Papa's eyebrows lifted. He looked at Mama, seated next to him. "Teacher Rhoda is probably missing all the children," he said. "I think it would be nice to spend an afternoon at her house. And a taffy pull sounds like fun. Hope you'll save a piece for me."

"We will," Joseph and Lily said at the same time.

Lily wished today was the day for the taffy pull. Seven whole days was a long time to wait for something so exciting.

Lily woke to the sound of raindrops splashing against her window. She jumped out of bed and ran to the window. What a disappointment! She had high hopes for a brilliantly sunny day. Today was the day for Teacher Rhoda's taffy pull party.

Papa and Mama weren't at all alarmed by the chance of rain ruining this special day. They chatted while they ate breakfast and didn't even talk about the weather.

Lily could hardly pick at her food. Too worried to eat. "Do you think it will rain all day?"

"There's an old saying about rain," Papa said. "Rain before seven. Quit before eleven." He looked at the clock. "It's not quite seven yet so I don't think you have to be worried about it raining all day long."

Lily brightened. Her appetite suddenly returned and she

finished her breakfast in three or four big gulps. Then she had to wait, tapping her toes, until everyone else was done.

First, Lily needed to help Mama with the Saturday cleaning. She kept one eye on the window to see if the rain was stopping. By nine o'clock, a streak of sunlight broke through the heavy gray clouds and Lily felt quite cheerful. But then, heavy fog rolled in. How terrible! Fog was worse than rain. So eerie and gloomy.

After lunch, Papa told Joseph and Lily to change their clothes while he went to the barn to hitch Jim to the buggy. Lily didn't even have to do dishes today. She bolted upstairs to her room to change. In a flash, she was back downstairs. Mama checked Joseph and Lily's hands and faces before they ran out the door and hopped in the buggy. They both sat on the front seat next to Papa. Jim trotted down the road, and Papa whistled merrily. The fog swirled around them and she wondered how Jim knew where the road lay. She looked up at Papa. "Have you ever been to a taffy pull?"

"I've been to a few," Papa said. "I think you'll enjoy it."

"What do you do?" Joseph asked.

"Rhoda will cook sugar into taffy," Papa said. "As soon as it's cool enough to touch, she'll divide it into pieces. It will look a little like a rope. Everyone pairs up to pull and pull and pull the ropes until it's ready to eat." He grinned. "When I used to go to taffy pulls, the boys paired with the girls."

Lily's eyes went wide in horror, so Papa quickly added, "I doubt Rhoda would have you do that."

Lily let out a big breath of relief. Papa turned Jim into the driveway that led to Samuel and Rhoda's house. As Lily and Joseph climbed out of the buggy, he said, "Be good and have fun. I'll be back around four o'clock to pick you up."

He waited to drive away until Lily knocked on the door and Teacher Rhoda invited them inside.

A whiff of sweet vanilla and caramel floated past the open door. Lily smiled. Even dreary fog couldn't ruin that smell.

Teacher Rhoda hurried back to the stove and stirred a pot of bubbling taffy. Joseph and Lily were the first to arrive and peeked around the house. Everything looked new and shiny, but not cozy. Not yet. A row of chairs and several benches lined the walls in the living room. A sewing machine was tucked in the corner.

A few children started to drift into the house: Beth and her brother Reuben, Hannah and Levi. Everyone stood around, acting stiff and awkward. No one knew what to do. Teacher Rhoda was busy with the hot taffy on the stove. Effie arrived, followed by Aaron Yoder and his brother Ezra. Disappointing! Lily had secretly hoped they might not be able to come today. Soon, the little house seemed to be bursting with children.

Teacher Rhoda handed butter to the oldest girls and asked them to spread it on the table. Lily watched as they coated the table with slippery butter. Lily was shocked! She had spread butter with her fingers on the bottom of cake and bread pans, but never a tabletop. She started to imagine what it would be like at home to have butter on the table. Dishes would slip right off and crash on the floor! Wouldn't Paul and Dannie be surprised by that?

Teacher Rhoda poured the hot taffy onto the table to cool. As soon as it was cool enough to touch, she had the children coat their hands with butter while she cut the taffy into ropes. She asked everyone to pair up and handed a rope to each twosome. She showed them how to pull it and then

fold it back together before pulling it again. Pull and fold. Pull and fold.

Lily and Beth were a pair—so were Hannah and Malinda. Effie had paired up with one of the bigger girls, whom she preferred because she thought they were more mature than girls her own age. Across the room, the boys laughed loudly as they pulled their taffy as far as they could before folding it back together. Lily was sure they were going to get some stuck to the floor before the day was over.

"I'm glad we're pulling taffy together," Lily whispered to Beth. "Papa said when he used to go to taffy pulls the boys had to pair up with the girls."

Effie overheard and her eyes twinkled with mischief. "Teacher Rhoda, Lily thought of a good idea. Can we pair up with the boys like the youth do at taffy pulls?"

Lily's mouth dropped in an O. How awful!

"How many of you would like to do that?" Teacher Rhoda asked.

A chorus of "We do!" sang out from the girls, drowning out Lily's "Not me!"

"It could be fun for a little while," Teacher Rhoda said.

Effie dropped her end of the taffy and hurried across the room to Aaron Yoder. "I'll pull taffy with you," she said eagerly.

Hannah bolted in front of her. "No! I get to pull with Aaron."

The two girls glared at each other while Aaron calmly ignored them and kept on pulling his taffy with Sam Stoltzfus. Effie reached in and grabbed one end of the taffy as Sam folded it up to Aaron's end.

Teacher Rhoda stepped in. "Hold on, girls. I'll write the boys' names on a piece of paper and put them in a bowl. Each girl can draw a name."

Effie squinted her little mean squint at Hannah. Hannah spun around and walked away. Neither one liked Teacher Rhoda's solution. Lily didn't either. She was furious. Why did she ever say anything about Papa to Beth? Everyone was having fun until Effie opened her big mouth. She hoped she would draw Joseph's name. Or Cousin Levi's.

But when it was her turn to draw a name, she reached into the bowl for a little piece of paper, opened it, and read: "Aaron Yoder." How awful! How terrible. She should have known this day was going to turn out badly—first the rain, then the fog, and now . . . *this*!

Everyone started to pair up. Lily waited miserably until Aaron was the only person without a partner. She made her feet move across the room to join him. She expected to see him stick his tongue out at her like he always did at school. Surprisingly, he didn't.

Effie gave Lily one of her mean squinty looks. She was partnered with a little second grader named Leroy. Instead of pulling the taffy, she practically jerked it out of poor Leroy's hands. He was terrified of her.

"I don't know why you always have to get the best things," Effie said to Lily.

The best thing? Aaron Yoder? "We can trade," Lily said.

Effie tossed the taffy at poor Leroy and flounced over to Aaron. But he would have none of getting traded off. He held the taffy behind his back. "I think we should stay with the names we drew," he said. "It's only fair."

Since when did Aaron Yoder ever worry about being fair? Lily wasn't sure what to do next. Neither was Leroy. He held a big ball of taffy in his hands, trembling like a leaf.

Calm as a cucumber, Aaron offered Lily the other end of the rope of taffy so she went back to pulling it. Pull and fold. Pull and fold.

But Effie wasn't so easily fobbed off. Her eyes narrowed into angry little slits. She grabbed the ball of soft taffy out of Leroy's hands and smashed it down on Lily's head. For a moment that felt like an hour, Lily stood there, stunned. Then she dropped the taffy she was pulling on with Aaron and tried to remove the gooey taffy from her hair and prayer covering. She was a mess.

Tears filled Lily's eyes. She had been so excited about this day, and it was turning into a disaster. Teacher Rhoda hurried over to help Lily get the taffy off her head. "Effie, go sit on one of the chairs in the living room," she said. Effie scowled and marched into the living room. She sat on a chair where she could still watch what was going on with the rest of the children.

Teacher Rhoda did the best she could, but she finally gave up trying to clean all the taffy out of Lily's hair. "You'll have to wash your hair as soon as you get home tonight."

Soon, it was time to cut the taffy into little pieces. Teacher Rhoda put the pieces into sandwich baggies so everyone could take some home with them. Lily was relieved to see Papa's buggy drive up to the house. His eyebrows lifted curiously when he saw the tufts of taffy stuck in her hair, but he could tell she didn't want to talk about it and he didn't ask.

Besides, he didn't have to. Joseph gave him the entire blow-by-blow story, all the way home. Lily stared out the buggy window. The fog was gone now and the sky was clearing. Why had she worried about the weather? It didn't matter what kind of weather the day held. She had worried about the wrong thing. As long as Effie Kauffman was around, every day was a continual worry.

Effie's Quilt Block

On Saturday morning, Lily tossed the end of a rug over the porch railing and shook the dirt off. She flipped it back over to shake the other side. She heard a horse clip-clopping down the road, so she stopped to see if she knew who was passing by. To her delight, the buggy turned into her driveway. Beth waved to her from the front seat, next to her mother.

Lily tossed the rug on the floor and ran down the porch steps to meet them. Alice Raber got off the buggy and reached under the seat to get the tie rope for the horse. Beth hopped off the buggy, a paper bag in her hands. She ran over to Lily while Alice tied the horse to the hitching post. "We're making a quilt for Teacher Rhoda," she said.

Lily eyed the little brown paper bag. It didn't look big enough to hold a quilt.

"Is your mother at home?" Beth's mother asked.

"Yes," Lily said. "She's in the kitchen scrubbing the stove top." Lily was happy to be outside for that chore. Rubbing the metal made a screechy sound that set Lily's teeth on edge.

Lily ran ahead of them and held the kitchen door open. "Alice and Beth are here."

Mama wiped her hands on her apron and hurried to the door. "Come in, come in!"

"We don't have time to stay long," Alice said. "We're stopping at all the families with schoolchildren and dropping off quilt blocks. We want to make a memory quilt for Teacher Rhoda as a thank-you for her years of teaching school."

Beth handed the little paper bag to Mama.

Mama opened it and drew out two quilt blocks.

"If you could embroider Lily and Joseph's names on the blocks and get them back to me by the end of the month," Alice said, "I'll sew all the blocks together. Then I'll have a quilting for all the mothers to get it quilted."

"What a nice idea," Mama said. "We'll start on these quilt blocks as soon as we're finished with the Saturday cleaning."

Alice and Beth left to deliver the rest of the quilt blocks. Lily picked up a rug to shake it with renewed energy. Shaking rugs was much more fun if there was something to look forward to.

Mama spread the two quilt blocks on the table and handed a pencil to Lily and Joseph. "Write your names as neatly as you can," she said, "and then I'll start embroidering them." Mama held the sides of Joseph's quilt block to keep it from moving while he labored at trying to write his name as neatly as possible. Lily tried writing the L for her name but the fabric moved so she sat and waited until Mama was finished helping Joseph.

251

It was hard to write on fabric. Lily worked carefully until she had written Lily Lapp in big neat letters across the middle of the quilt block. "Can I draw a flower in the corners?"

"I think that might look nice," Mama said. She held the fabric while Lily carefully drew flowers in each of the corners. They looked like little impatiens.

Mama found two embroidery hoops in her sewing closet and fastened the fabric in them. "You can embroider your name with a chain stitch while I do Joseph's," Mama said. "And then I'll show you how to do the flowers."

Chain stitch was Lily's favorite way to embroider, and she set to work making neat, small chains. She worked on the quilt block every evening after supper. She was pleased with it and thought her quilt patch would be the prettiest of all the ones in the quilt.

It wasn't long before both quilt blocks were finished. Mama folded them carefully and put them into a big brown envelope. She let Lily write Alice Raber's address on it and carry it to the mailbox. Lily hoped Alice would start sewing the blocks together right away. She couldn't wait until the quilting.

Church was at Effie Kauffman's house on a Sunday morning in mid-August. Lily didn't mind going to Effie's for church nearly as much as she minded having Effie to church at her house. When Effie's family hosted church, she was in charge, and when she was in charge, she was happy.

After the service, Lily and her friends were visiting in Effie's bedroom. The girls were looking through Effie's big collection of books on a shelf above her bed. Lily couldn't believe how many books Effie had. They all looked interesting.

"Maybe we could read," Lily suggested. Reading was her favorite thing to do.

"No," Effie said. "I already read those books."

But Lily hadn't! Neither had the other girls.

"Let's play communion," Effie said. "I'll go downstairs and get everything we need."

As soon as Effie had disappeared, Hannah said, "I wonder why Effie thinks we're not too big to play communion."

Beth nodded. "She thinks we're getting too big to do almost everything we used to after church when we were still little girls."

Everyone agreed, but no one volunteered to tell Effie they didn't want to play communion. That was the thing about Effie. Somehow, she always got her way. No one dared to disagree with her—at least, not to her face.

Effie came back upstairs with several slices of bread and a glass of water. There was a strange lump in her dress pocket that showed through her apron. "What do you have in your pocket?" Lily asked. She just knew this was a bad idea.

"Since you need to know everything, it's my handkerchief," Effie said, eyes narrowed. She turned to Malinda, who did whatever she said. "You can be the preacher and hand out the bread and water."

Everyone lined up beside the bed. Malinda broke bits of bread off the slice she held in her hand and gave one to each of the girls.

When each girl sat on the bed, Effie said, "Now it's my turn to be the preacher, but this time let's do something different. Everyone stand with your eyes closed and your mouth wide open, and I'll put the piece of bread right into your mouth."

Just like always, everyone followed Effie's orders. Lily

wished someone would tell her that her games were dumb. Someone besides Lily.

"Okay, here I come," Effie said. Lily held her hands behind her back and stood with her eyes closed tightly and her mouth open. Effie started down the line, dropping a piece of bread in each girl's mouth. Lily was at the end of the line. All of a sudden, Beth and Malinda and Hannah started to cough and spit. Lily's eyes flew open and she clamped her mouth shut. Effie had sprinkled the bread pieces with cayenne pepper. She laughed and laughed as the girls ran to the bathroom, gagging.

Lily felt sorry for her friends. She ran to see if she could help them. They were trying to rinse their mouths with water. Tears were streaming down their flushed faces.

"It hurts so bad," Beth said, gasping between gulps of water.

Lily was worried about Beth—her piece of bread had more pepper on it than Hannah's or Malinda's. She ran downstairs to get Beth's mother. Alice Raber hurried up the stairs to the bathroom.

"Make the burning stop, Mama!" Beth cried when she saw her mother.

"What on earth happened?" Alice said.

Everyone looked at Effie. "Effie told us to open our mouth and close our eyes and then she gave us bread sprinkled with cayenne pepper," Lily said.

Ida Kauffman came upstairs to see what was happening and heard what Lily had said. Effie, now deflated, looked smaller.

"Clearly, these girls need to be watched more closely," Ida said. "Whenever they're together, they seem to create mischief." She gave Lily a look as if she probably started the whole thing.

"Beth, let's go downstairs and get something to relieve the burning," Alice said.

Hands on her hips, Ida frowned at Hannah, Malinda, and Lily. "And now the rest of you go down and sit by your mothers for the rest of the afternoon."

No one dared to speak up to her. Lily wanted to, though. She wanted to point out that Effie was the one who created 99 percent of the mischief. Did Ida realize that? But of course, she didn't say anything. Being rude to a grown-up was worse than being falsely accused.

Teacher Rhoda would be very pleased, though, to know that Lily had used some arithmetic in real life—a percentage—without it being an assignment.

Lily, Hannah, and Malinda went down to the kitchen and quietly slipped onto benches next to their mothers. All except Effie. She went outside to play with the older girls.

An hour or so later, the families started to head home for evening chores. Lily saw Ida Kauffman take an envelope and hand it to Effie. "Tuck that in Beth or Alice's bonnet," she told her. "Don't let Rhoda see you."

Lily and Mama helped gather the last of the dishes and put them in the kitchen sink. By the time Papa had brought Jim up to the door, their two bonnets were the only ones left. Lily put her bonnet over her prayer cap and tied the ribbons. A pin poked her head and she loosened the ties. She did not like her big bonnet.

When everyone returned home, Lily took her bonnet off and hung it on the wall peg. Something fluttered out and landed on the floor. Lily picked it up. Why, it wasn't a pin that had poked her. It was an envelope. Effie had put her quilt square in the wrong bonnet!

"Lily, come help me get supper ready," Mama called from the kitchen.

Lily opened the envelope and looked at the quilt square: "EFFIE" it said in big, fat letters. Nothing else. Just her giant-sized name. And wasn't that typical of Effie?

Lily stood there awhile, wondering what to do with the quilt square. The right thing to do would be to tell Mama right away so Effie's quilt square would get to Alice in time to be included in the quilt. That would be the right thing to do.

But then Lily thought about all the mean things Effie had done to her: the sandwich switch, the taffy pull, even today—putting cayenne pepper on bread.

She crumbled up the envelope, tucked the quilt square into her dress pocket, and went to help Mama with supper.

The Quilting

A few weeks later, a postcard arrived in the mail to invite Mama and Lily to the quilting.

"It looks like we're going to have a very busy week," Mama said. "We have a lot of canning and garden work to do. But if we work extra hard, we should be able to make it to the quilting."

For once, Lily didn't mind helping Mama with the garden work. Lily liked quiltings. She could visit with her friends, and Mama could visit with her friends. Everyone laughed a lot, and delicious food was served. Going to a quilting would be a fun change.

Every now and then, she felt a pinch of guilt about Effie's quilt block, hidden in her room. She quickly dismissed it when she imagined Effie's face as the quilt was given to Teacher Rhoda and her quilt block was missing. Nowhere to be seen. Effie would be furious! And it wasn't Lily's fault, she told herself. She didn't purposely take that quilt block. Effie was the one who put it in the wrong bonnet.

The night before the quilting, Lily fell asleep quickly but woke with a start. She had been having a nightmare that Effie found her quilt square hidden in Lily's room and Ida sent Lily off to jail. She tiptoed into Mama's room and tapped her on the shoulder.

"Lily?" Mama said, startled. "What's wrong? Are you sick?"

"No," Lily whispered, and mumbled the truth.

"What?" Mama said.

Lily hoped Papa wouldn't wake up. "I did something I shouldn't." She held out Effie's quilt square. A beam of moonlight shone right on it.

Mama listened carefully to Lily's story, then told her to go back to bed. "We'll talk about it in the morning."

Lily overslept in the morning and had to hurry when Mama woke her to say it was time to leave for the quilting. Papa had already hitched Jim to the buggy and handed the reins to Mama. Lily felt sorry for the boys as she climbed on the front seat next to Mama. The boys would stay at home with Papa today. Boys did not belong at a quilting.

Jim trotted through the cool morning air. Normally, Lily loved summer mornings when the air still had a bite to it, almost chilly. The days were warm but mornings were always nice. Today, though, she felt too guilty to enjoy anything.

Mama didn't say anything for a long time. Lily started to hope that maybe she had forgotten about what Lily said in the night. Maybe . . . Mama thought she was dreaming!

"Lily, Aufgeschoben ist nicht aufgehoben" *Omission is not acquittance.*

Lily had no idea what that meant. In Penn Dutch or in English.

"Not telling the truth about the quilt square is the same thing as lying."

Oh. *Oh!*

Mama's face softened. "I know that Effie is not an easy friend to have. But two wrongs never make a right."

Jonas Raber was waiting in the barnyard to take care of the horses as the women drove up. Jonas unhitched Jim from the buggy and led him into the barn where he could eat hay until it was time to go home again. At least Jim would be happy.

In the house, Mama and Lily removed their bonnets and placed them on a bench. Mama checked to make sure Lily's covering was straight and tied neatly. Then they went to the living room where the quilt top was set up, ready for quilting. Lily noticed that every student's quilt block was set in place. All except Effie's. Her stomach twisted inside and out.

Lily and Beth sat behind the quilt. They were too little to quilt but they could measure the thread in yard lengths and thread a lot of needles for the mothers. Beth asked why Lily was extra quiet but she only shrugged. She was waiting for Effie and Ida to notice that Effie's quilt block was missing. Worse still, what if Mama asked Lily to confess in front of everyone? Lily felt like she was waiting for a thunderstorm to hit. Amazingly, no one seemed to notice.

When it was time to make lunch, Alice Raber asked the girls to help her. Lily, Beth, and Hannah set the table while Effie helped Alice prepare the food. Naturally, Effie volunteered for the most important job.

It wasn't long before lunch was ready. Alice had made a creamy potato soup and cute chicken salad sandwiches. She

filled a bowl with soup and a small tray with sandwiches and asked Beth and Lily to take it out to Jonas Raber in the barn. "He doesn't want to come inside," Alice told the girls. "He said that it was better to let the women cluck all they wanted to without a man getting in their way."

After lunch was over, Alice rinsed the food bits off the dishes and fixed the dishwater. "I think we'll let the little girls wash the dishes," she said, and Lily's heart sank. There were piles and piles of dirty dishes!

Malinda rolled up her sleeves and started to slowly wash dishes. Lily rinsed. She made the plates float and twirl on the rinse water before putting them into the drainer for Hannah and Effie to dry. Beth put the dishes away, since she knew where everything belonged.

"I wish we never had to wash dishes again," Hannah said.

"Me too," all the other girls chimed together.

"You know what I feel like doing with them?" Malinda said.

"What?"

"I would like to hang them out on the clothesline and shoot them with a big rifle," Malinda said.

The girls looked at Malinda in surprise, then they burst out laughing. Malinda was usually quiet. She didn't come up with ideas like that. Effie did, but Malinda didn't.

Then all the girls thought up things they would like to do with dirty dishes. Lily said they could be buried in the garden. Hannah thought it would be fun to float them down the creek. Beth said she thought everyone should use paper plates—that would solve the whole problem.

They got so involved in their imaginings that the dishes were washed and dried in the blink of an eye. The girls put the last dish away and hurried outside to play. Lily had almost forgotten about Effie's missing quilt block. Almost.

By late afternoon, most of the quilt had been quilted and Alice said that she could finish it up by herself. Everyone oohed and aahed as they stood back and admired the beautiful quilt.

And then it hit. Suddenly Effie let out a wail. "Where's my quilt block?"

"Oh dear," Alice said, distressed. "I don't think I ever got one from you."

Ida started hunting up and down the rows for it. "Effie, didn't you put the envelope I gave you into Beth's bonnet?"

"I did! I did!" Effie said. "I know I did." She started to cry. Lily's belly clenched with a sick dread.

Mama went to the front door and came back with a shopping bag. She handed the bag to Effie. "Effie," Mama said, "you must have put the envelope with your quilt block into the wrong bonnet at church."

Over Lily's head, Mama gave her one of her direct looks. Lily felt tears prickle her eyes. She would not cry! She wouldn't. She had to be brave.

"It's an easy mistake to make," Mama said. "The bonnets all look alike. But I just discovered your quilt block and it was too late for Alice to add it into the quilt top. So I turned it into a pillow for Teacher Rhoda."

Effie pulled the pillow out of the bag and gasped. Mama had made a beautiful quilted pillow top, with Effie's big square right in the middle of it, surrounded by small quilted pieces. Effie's face lit up. "This can go on top of the quilt!" She looked around the room at Lily and Beth and Hannah and Malinda. "It can go on top of everyone else's quilt blocks." She gave the girls a smug smile. "Everyone's." Even Ida seemed pleased.

That was all that Mama said about the quilt block. Nothing more to Ida, to Effie, or to Lily. The subject was closed. The lesson was learned.

On the way home, Lily scooted close to Mama and rested her head on her shoulder. She had the best mother in the world.

Alice Raber planned to give Teacher Rhoda the quilt on Sunday, right after church. The rest of the week passed so slowly. Finally, Sunday arrived. After the church service and fellowship meal, Alice gathered all the schoolchildren into a bedroom. She arranged the boys along one side of the quilt and the girls along the other side, then she went to get Teacher Rhoda.

A few minutes later, Teacher Rhoda popped her head into the bedroom. She looked puzzled when she saw all the children lined up. "Surprise!" they shouted.

"We wanted to make a memory quilt for you as a little symbol of appreciation for all the years of teaching you did," Alice said.

Tears started to stream down Teacher Rhoda's cheeks. Lily was surprised. She had never seen Teacher Rhoda cry. "I don't know how to thank all of you," she said, stroking the quilt gently and looking at each square. "I enjoyed my years of teaching and I will treasure this beautiful quilt always."

Lily was pleased to see her block near the top middle of the quilt. She thought it really was the prettiest one. Then Effie pulled out the pillow Mama had made with her quilt block on it. "Here's the best part," Effie said, plopping it right on top of Lily's quilt block. Teacher Rhoda was delighted and said it was just the right finishing touch to a beautiful quilt.

Somehow, Lily thought, Effie always ended up getting what she wanted. But as for the best part—Lily knew that wasn't true. The best part was having a family like the one Lily had. The best part was having friends she could trust like Hannah and Beth and Malinda.

The best part, Lily knew, wasn't a thing.

Questions about
the Old Order Amish

Lily's family lived on a farmette—but what is a farmette?
A farm is a large acreage with enough land to raise crops.
Eighty acres is considered a small farm. Whispering Pines,
Lily's farmette, was only fifteen acres; there was some land
for pastures and animals but it wasn't big enough to be considered a farm. Those small acreages are called farmettes.

Do the Amish make their own clothing? Yes, just like Lily's
mother, the lady of the house sews the clothes for herself
and her family. A lot of sewing is done in the winter, when
the garden is sleeping and field harvest is over. The mother
makes dresses, aprons, capes, and coverings for herself and
her daughters. She sews pants and shirts for her husband and
boys. Most Amish women use the treadle sewing machine,
though some may use battery-powered sewing machines. Did
it surprise you to read that Lily's grown-up dress and apron
were held together with pins? Actual long straight pins! It

might seem odd, but Amish women and girls are used to it. It's a tradition.

Do the Amish wear colored clothes? They do. The women wear shades of blue, green, red, purple, brown, etc. Most colors are darker tones of the color wheel. Men wear colored shirts—white on Sunday or for funerals or weddings. Pants are navy blue, gray, or black. Little boys and girls may wear lighter shades of the above colors.

What is a circle letter? When Lily turned ten, her mother told her she was old enough for her own circle letter. Letter writing is a popular pastime for the Amish. It's one way they stay in touch with relatives, exchange advice, and maintain community. But what is a circle letter? It's a communal letter that is added to and then sent on to the next recipient on a list. Circle letters may be maintained by grown siblings, friends, cousins, or groups with similar interests, such as teachers or quilters.

What is courting? Courting is another word for dating, though it is meant to lead to marriage. Family is at the heart of Amish life, and young people take courtship seriously. For many of the Old Order Amish young people, "pairing up" begins at Sunday evening singings. The boy will take the girl home in his buggy. Courting is very private. Most couples don't want to be teased, so they make a great effort to keep their dates secret.

What is an Amish wedding like? About two weeks before the wedding, the engaged couple is "published" in church and their intentions to marry are made known. Most weddings are held on Tuesdays and Thursdays. Mondays, Wednesdays, and Fridays are used as days to prepare for or to clean up after the wedding. Saturdays are not used as wedding days because it would be breaking the Sabbath to clean up on the following day, Sunday.

The wedding is held at the home of the bride, and the sermon and ceremony will last about four hours, starting at 8:30 a.m. There are no kisses, rings, photography, flowers, or caterers. There are usually 200 or more guests. The bride's family furnishes all the food. Women from the community help with preparation in the days before the wedding, and aunts of both the bride and groom are assigned to help cook on the wedding day. After the wedding, there will be a traditional dinner of chicken, filling, mashed potatoes, gravy, ham, relishes, and canned fruit, plus many kinds of cookies, cakes, and pies. And Sweetheart Pudding!

Were you interested in trying a taste of the pudding that was served at Rhoda and Samuel's wedding? The recipe is on the next page.

Sweetheart Pudding

    4 cups milk
    1½ cups sugar
    3 egg yolks
    4 tablespoons flour
    1 teaspoon vanilla

Mix all ingredients together in a saucepan and bring to a full boil. Cool.

    3 cups graham cracker crumbs
    ½ cup butter
    ¼ cup sugar
    1 cup sugared pecans (see recipe that follows)

In a large mixing bowl, combine graham cracker crumbs, butter, and sugar. In a clear serving bowl, layer one cup of graham crumb mixture and press firmly. Add half of cooled pudding. Toss sugared nuts and one cup of graham cracker mixture together and layer on top of pudding. Add rest of pudding. Sprinkle top with remaining cup of graham cracker mixture. Refrigerate.

To make sugared nuts:

    1 egg white
    1 tablespoon water
    2 cups coarsely chopped pecans
    ½ cup sugar
    1½ teaspoons cinnamon
    ¼ teaspoon salt

In a mixing bowl, beat egg white and water until fluffy. Fold in chopped pecans. In a small bowl, combine sugar, cinnamon, and salt. Sprinkle over pecans and toss until coated. Spread on lightly greased baking sheet and bake at 225° for 1 hour, stirring every 15 minutes. Cool and store in airtight container.

Note from Lily: Sugared nuts are good for Sweetheart Pudding and also for snacking.

Mary Ann Kinsinger was raised Old Order Amish in Somerset County, Pennsylvania. She met and married her husband, whom she knew from school days, and started a family. After they chose to leave the Amish church, Mary Ann began a blog, *A Joyful Chaos*, as a way to capture her warm memories of her childhood for her own children. From the start, this blog found a ready audience and even captured the attention of key media players, such as the influential blog *Amish America* and the *New York Times*. She lives in Pennsylvania.

Suzanne Woods Fisher's grandfather was one of eleven children, raised Old Order German Baptist, in Franklin County, Pennsylvania. Suzanne has many, many, *many* wonderful Plain relatives. She has written bestselling fiction and nonfiction books about the Amish and couldn't be happier to share Mary Ann's stories with children. When Suzanne isn't writing, she is raising puppies for Guide Dogs for the Blind. She lives in California with her husband and children and Tess and Toffee, her big white dogs.